The Legend of Grizzly Adams and Kodiak Jack

By the Same Author

FICTION BOOK SERIES
New Classics for the Twenty-First Century
Dorothy—Return to Oz

The Days of Laura Ingalls Wilder
Missouri Homestead; Children of Promise
Good Neighbors; Home to the Prairie
The World's Fair; Mountain Miracle
The Great Debate; Land of Promise

The Younguns
Younguns of Mansfield, Missouri
Frankie and the Secret; Escape From Barron Stoker
Orphan of the Ozarks

NONFICTION
Death at Chappaquiddick

Other FamilyVision Series You Would Enjoy
Shivers
Vampire Island

Dino Mites
Dino Mites Declare War!; School's Out Forever!

Troll Family Adventures
Kidnapped to the Center of the Earth; Lost in LA!

The Adventures of Shelly Holmes
Dead Man's Confession

The Patti Pinkerton Mystery Series
Trouble at The Cave

Petz
Chili Dogs

GRIZZLY ADAMS AND KODIAK JACK™

Book One

The Legend of
Grizzly Adams and Kodiak Jack

Thomas L. Tedrow

FamilyVision Press

New York

FamilyVision Press™
For The Family That Reads Together™
An imprint of Multi Media Communicators, Inc.
575 Madison Avenue, Suite 1006
New York, NY 10022

Cover, Lou Grant
Typesetter, Samuel Chapin

Library of Congress Catalog Card Number: 93-071555

ISBN 1-56969-050-2

10 9 8 7 6 5 4 3 2 1
First Edition

Printed in the United States of America

63409

To my wife Carla who helped me see God's path in the
pathless forest: You gave me the courage
to share my stories with the world.

To my children C.T., Tyler, Tara, and Travis:
You opened the magic world of childhood in my mind.

To my mother, Gertrude Tedrow:
You taught me faith, courage, kindness,
love and understanding.

To my late father, Richard Tedrow:
You told me I could be anything I wanted.
I miss you every day.

On his deathbed Grizzly Adams said, "I have looked on death in many forms and I trust that I can meet it whenever it comes, with a stout heart and steady nerves."

He was the bravest mountain man of them all.

Introduction

I can remember the first time I heard about Grizzly Adams. Just the memory of that evening beside a crackling campfire, the sounds of night just outside the glow, brings back the tingle.

Though I'm a long way from that twelve-year-old boy at Scout camp, the troop leader's words are still with me. "I'm going to tell you a story about the greatest mountain man of them all. His name was Grizzly Adams."

Grizzly Adams? Just the name made us all move closer together in anticipation of a campfire story. I raised my hand and asked, "Are you talking about a man or a bear?"

The troop leader smiled. "I'm going to tell you a story about the man who lived with the grizzly bears and the Indians. About a man who loved the woods more than he loved people. About a man who had so much courage that he was braver than Kit Carson, Davy Crockett and Daniel Boone combined."

Then he told an incredible story about this shoemaker from Massachusetts who decided to change his life and challenge himself. We sat mesmerized; the story about this bearded mountain man who had a strange power over bears and animals coming alive in our minds.

We could hear the scream of the bobcats, the explosions of Kentucky rifles and could see a twelve-inch bear track with two missing toes in the snow. My heart raced with excitement as we followed the bear tracks through the snowy woods in our minds, fighting off renegades and wolves.

Our city lives seemed to pale in comparison to living in the mountains, defending your honor and being self-reliant. Thrown in for good measure was the troop leader's belief that Grizzly Adams and the men and women like him were what made America great. That these pioneer Americans who didn't believe in defeat, made this country what it is.

That fireside story came back to me as I looked at the newspaper headlines: Drugs sweeping America, violence in our schools, and our institutions under assault. Where are the role models? What happened to America?

I thought about that scoutmaster's campfire tale and finally understood what he gave me. Sitting by the campfire, listening to the sounds of night, the scoutmaster painted me images of a time and place that made America great, images that have stayed with me and influenced my life in countless ways.

About duty, honor and country. About standing up for what's right, defending the weak and not being afraid to go against the crowd. Like Grizzly Adams and the other trailblazers who opened up America.

So I decided to open up those trails to a new generation and set out to create a legend about Grizzly Adams and Kodiak Jack. I hope this story stirs you as much as that crackling campfire tale did for me.

Thomas L. Tedrow
Winter Park, Florida

CONTENTS

Introduction

The Legend of Grizzly Adams
and Kodiak Jack

CHAPTER ONE

How the Legend Began

California Sierras, 1852

A bearded, muscular man pushed his two-yoked oxen harder, but it was no use. Even with the nip in the fall air, the animals were about as beat as the battered wagon they pulled.

James Capen Adams was a long way from the town of Medway, Massachusetts, but in his mind he was not far enough. Behind him lay a string of broken dreams. Ahead lay the edge of civilization which he was intent on crossing, to live in the wilderness with the grizzlies and mountain lions.

"Money's for fools," he called out to the oxen, who didn't raise an ear between them. "I'll make my way in spite of the world."

He thought of how the men had laughed when he told them he was going to be a mountain man. "I'll show 'em all that it's the man that's the mountain man, not the buckskins." Then he looked down at the ill-fitting butternut-cloth miner's clothes he had on. "'Course, I'll be needin' some new clothes out here. Ain't never seen a mountain man in store-bought clothes."

He would have cracked a whip if he'd had one, to put distance between himself and the courts which had taken everything he owned in the world, but he knew that the poor oxen couldn't go any faster. "You're a mighty poor excuse of a team," he laughed, "the most sorry beasts I've ever seen."

The few wagons he passed received no more than a grunted hello, for Adams was in no mood for human company. "The bigger the mouth, the better it looks shut if you ask me," he muttered under his breath, as a big, strapping German shouted a greeting. "Just don't turn back this way," he mumbled, hoping that his nearest neighbor wouldn't be any closer than the farthest one away.

America had been settled by wild men like himself, men not afraid to challenge the world. "But they's changin' things," Adams complained to the oxen who answered with a swat of their tails. "Doin' everythin' for the lawyers and nothin' for those that work hard."

The one man he still respected was Ben Franklin, a man he'd only read about, but Ben Franklin was dead and so was the life that Adams was escaping. But as he left the oaks and ash trees behind, as the air cleared and the chill of approaching winter touched him, his mood changed.

As they climbed higher into the mountains, the digger pines and chaparral replaced the grassland. Toyon, the native holly of the Californias, appeared and the small animals who spied on him from the edge of the trail were proof that he was leaving behind all that he despised.

It was his dream of escaping the stifling life of Boston and the East that had driven Adams through the tough times. Though he'd failed in a dozen ventures of every description, it was the dream that gave him the strength and courage to get up and try again.

With just two rifles, one a Kentucky and one a

Tennessee, a battered five-shot Colt pistol and a Hudson Bay Point blanket to his name, James Capen Adams was prepared to forsake his past life and live in the wild Sierras. He was ready to leave civilization behind.

It wasn't the first time that Adams had tried to escape. When he was twenty-one, he put down his shoemaker tools and joined a New Hampshire zoo company as an animal trapper until he was mauled by a tiger and almost died. All he could do was go back to making shoes.

But he never forgot the dream of chasing his destiny in the uncharted territories, of living with the wild animals and Indians.

So for fifteen years he'd worked, bent over on his shoemaker's bench, pounding with his hammer on the soles of others' shoes. Each nail went in like the last and was no different than the next. But the dream kept him going as he hammered countless shoes until he'd saved six thousand dollars, enough for a stake.

Investing the money in shoes to sell to pioneers heading west from St. Louis, James Capen Adams believed that he would triple his money. But luck was not with him: A fire raged through his shoe warehouse, taking everything he'd worked so hard to earn. Fifteen years of toil and sweat were gone.

Without a cent to his name, he worked his way west, nearly dying in Arizona, planning to earn enough money panning gold at Sutter's millrace at Coloma, California. To live in the wilderness, he needed a grubstake that would last the rest of his life.

But he lost the money he earned along the way in a failed mining claim which began a four-year string of bad luck. Each time he made enough working for others, he tried again to make his fortune, only to lose it all.

Failing as a miner, a gambler, a trader, a merchant, a grocery store manager and as a boarding house operator, Adams took any job he could find. He made shoes, dug mines, and cleaned barns. With his little savings, he borrowed enough to buy a fine herd of cattle only to have rustlers steal every single head.

Unable to pay his bills or loans, Adams was left with what the lawyers didn't want—two old percussion rifles, an ancient pistol, a blanket, wagon, and a team of broken-down oxen.

James Capen Adams rode off into the Sierras to live life on his terms, forsaking greed and the accumulation of money. "I'll wander, hunt, fish, and live life as I choose," he called out to the animals watching from the bushes.

At the end of the trail that separated civilization from the wilderness, Adams stopped and knelt down. "Lord, I'm in your hands. Ready to make my peace and live the rest of my life in the woods." He looked around, hearing nothing but the wind and birds. "I'll bother no one and ask for nothing. I'll trust only in You and in myself."

Calculating that he was about seventeen miles east of Sonora on a beautiful pine ridge between the Stanislaus River and the north fork of the Tuolumne River, he patted the ground, then stood.

"This is where I'm goin' to live. Right here. I'll be king of my own mountain," he laughed. He'd found the place that he would rule. No one would challenge him. Adams would set his own laws and live free or die.

That afternoon, while clearing his campsite, Adams saw an eagle flying erratically overhead. "Somethin' wrong with that bird," he said.

Later, he found the eagle sitting on the large rock that hung over the cliff near his campsite. There was a small, broken arrow sticking out from its side. Adams knew the eagle would die unless he helped it.

Taking a deep breath, Adams kept his eyes fixed on the eagle's as he moved slowly forward. "I won't hurt you, boy," he whispered. The eagle flapped its wings, then went calm as Adams carefully pulled the small tip out.

"Lucky for you it weren't barbed," he continued in a calming voice. "There you go," Adams said, tossing the arrow over the cliff.

The eagle flapped its wings, dancing around, then looked at Adams and lifted off. He watched the big eagle circling around, flying without a problem. "Now that's freedom," Adams sighed, watching the eagle dip down the sharp ravines.

Then the eagle swooped back up as if thanking Adams. "I'll call you Freedom," he said. "It's what we both got in common, I suppose."

It took him three weeks to build a log hut, chinking the cracks between the hand-hewn logs with clay from the granite ravines. He'd built it so the morning sun came through the front door. He'd put on a grass and sod roof and did as best he could to lay down a floor that butted into the stone chimney he'd made for cooking.

It had taken him and the two oxen half a day to pull a big flat stone from the river down below, which he laid as a doorstep. Next, he built an animal pen and then a smokehouse to cure his own meat. Behind the pen he put up an ash hopper in the yard to make soap. Adams figured that by mixing in the animal grease and fat from the game he hunted with the liquid lye he got from pouring water over hardwood ashes, that he'd make a regular supply of soap.

His first intruder was a raccoon he caught stealing food from the cutting board. "Hold on there, Bandit," Adams laughed. "You don't have to steal a thing," he said, tossing the raccoon some scraps.

Before the week was out, Bandit had become a regular houseguest, coming in and out of Adam's cabin as it pleased.

Everything Adams wanted came from the woods. He hunted game, dug for roots, picked berries, and shot his first buffalo in the flatlands below. Though he had never seen buffalo this side of the Platte, he knew that he'd need a warm coat for the winter.

He followed the buffalo, crawling through the tall grass, and when he got close enough he raised his Kentucky rifle and put a shot right behind the big animal's shoulder. The buffalo staggered several steps, then dropped straight down, its massive, curly head raising a cloud of dust.

Adams remembered what he'd learned back East and

pickled the skin with saltpeter, alum, and arsenic, which were the few chemicals he had brought in the wagon. "Got to keep it from stinkin'," he said, hoping to make the skin soft and pliable. It took several days of rubbing soaproot paste, scraping it off with a stone, and smoking the pelt to keep insects from damaging it. Within a week, he had a fine, thick coat.

What meat he didn't smoke, he loaded onto his oxen and took to trade with the Digger Indians, who he knew had been watching him from the woods. He found their village in the valley below and made peace over a feast of buffalo meat and bread made from grass seed and tule root, which they baked in the campfire's ashes.

From that point on they traded together, Adams bringing them venison for the winter hay he needed for his oxen. Then, at another feast, they presented him with his first set of buckskins, to replace his worn-out city clothes.

On the first morning he put on his new buckskins, he stood in front of the cabin, trying to admire himself. "What do you girls think?" he asked the two penned up oxen who just swatted their tails. "Well I think I look pretty darn good," he nodded. Bandit the raccoon stood on the rock doorstep covering his eyes with his paws. "I didn't ask you," Adams frowned.

The eagle he called Freedom hadn't been around for several days, but now it came swooping into the camp. It landed on top of the cabin, just staring at Adams.

"You hungry or what?" Adams said, preparing to get the eagle some scraps like he'd done before, but the eagle just flapped his wings then flew off.

Then he heard dogs barking in the distance—hunting dogs. "What are they doing here?" he said, irritated that he hadn't gone far enough in his journey to escape civilization. He'd come to regard the mountain as his. He was king of this mountain and wanted no intruders.

Hoping that they'd just go away, Adams busied himself feeding the oxen and the small deer that came around, trying not to listen to the baying dogs. "They better not come up here askin' for a handout. I don't want no people gettin' the idea of becomin' my neighbors."

Adams had hunted zoo animals for a menagerie company twenty years before back in New Hampshire and couldn't keep from listening to the dogs. He knew from their barks that they were nearing the end. They would soon corner whatever they were chasing.

"It's almost over," he said to Bandit, who scampered back into the cabin. Then he heard it—the barking that signaled the pack of hunting dogs had their prey trapped.

"Just finish your business and go," Adams grumbled, hoping that the hunters would take their catch and leave without bothering him anymore.

Then a loud roar echoed through the mountains followed by gunshots. "What the heck are they huntin'?" he wondered, walking over to the ledge that gave him a view of the valley below.

Now he could see it. A massive ghost-gray grizzly bear on the ridge in the distance was fighting for her life against a band of hunters. A small cub was behind her, trying to stay between its mother's legs.

The deer raced away and the oxen pushed at their pens, smelling the grizzly, wanting to escape. Grizzlies were the most feared animals in America and could gut an ox with one swipe of their powerful paws. Adams had caught bears before back East, but he'd never seen a bear the size of this one.

Adams grabbed his Kentucky rifle and ran off, unsure of what he was going to do. There were at least three hunters, white men he figured, but he was determined to stop them from killing the bear. They were on his mountain and he made the laws here.

CHAPTER TWO

Ben Franklin

It was hard to tell the animal from the men. The hunters wore massive bearskin jackets with fox-head hats. Their hair was long and scraggly, as were the fringed buckskins they wore.

The hounds were crazed, biting the sticks and bushes, trying to get at the big gray bear. They barked, howled, and moaned, dancing around, their nostrils flared. One charged forward, jumping up at the bear's neck, but the grizzly crushed her rib cage with a stunning blow, knocking the dog against the rocks. The grizzly spun around, her big eyes glowing red, ready to kill anything in her way.

The big bear swung around, then took a slow step forward as the other dogs charged. But the bear was ready and braced for the kill.

"Shoot her!" shouted a tall man with intense eyes. Around his neck were the teeth and claws from the many bears he'd killed.

One of the hunters raised his rifle, aiming at a spot near the base of the bear's throat, but the shot only grazed the bear. The big bear roared in pain, swinging at the air, pounding on the ground, trying to pull out the sting.

Adams moved forward cautiously. His sixth sense told him that there were other grizzlies around, but he wasn't sure where. It had been twenty-some years since he'd last been around big game and his senses were still citified.

"Watch out, Claw!" one of the hunters shouted to the

man with intense eyes. The savage grizzly stood upright and charged forward, killing another dog, its claws and teeth ripping the dog apart.

The man named Claw Wyler dodged the swinging paws, cradling his Sharps rifle like he had all the time in the world. Just one hit could rip the bear apart like a gutted hog. Adams watched, wondering what kind of game the man was playing.

Then he saw that one of the other men were taunting the big mother grizzly, holding her cub in front of her. A rage started to build inside Adams. *They shouldn't tease her.*

Claw turned his face to grin at the men behind him, not seeing the bear step forward. "Behind you!" shouted one of the hunters, who knelt down, taking aim.

The grizzly charged, smashing its paws down for the kill, breaking the man's neck with one swat, trying to get to her cub. "Toss the cub," Claw ordered, cocking his rifle.

The other hunter dropped the cub, which ran screaming into the bushes. Now there was just Claw and one other hunter left against the grizzly. The last dog jumped at the bear but was ripped apart.

There was no stopping the grizzly, crazed with pain and desperate to retrieve her cub. "Steady now," Claw said, taking aim. But the bear was too fast. She charged forward, knocking Claw to the ground.

The other hunter tried to help Claw get up but the bear caught the man with her claws, dragging him forward. Adams watched as the hunter died a gruesome death.

The bear charged toward Claw and with no time to aim, he shot from his hip toward the bear's open mouth. The bear dropped straight down.

"Got you in the brain," Claw grinned, figuring the bear was dead. But his aim was off.

The cub came out from the bushes, crying for its mother. Clay turned and walked toward the baby bear, not seeing the big bear rising. He had missed her mouth and just grazed her head.

Adams hesitated, wondering if he should get involved, then shouted, "Watch it!"

Claw turned towards Adams, just as the bear's paw came down on his face, nearly pulling off his left cheek. He screamed in agony, taking another shot, hitting the bear in the paw.

The enormous grizzly swung her bloody paw around, trying to shake away the pain. Claw had shot off two of her toes.

Adams walked forward, still cautious. He could feel it, smell it. There were other bears around, and probably other hunters, too.

The cub tried to nuzzle against its mother but she paid no attention. The mother charged forward again, knocking Claw down, then came at Adams.

"Back," Adams said. It was all he could think to say. Claw thought that Adams was going to be eaten alive, but the big bear stopped, inches away.

Adams concentrated on the bear's eyes, just as he'd learned to do back East, when he'd been able to catch animals without killing them. "I wish you no harm," he said calmly. The little cub ran between his legs and he stooped to pick it up.

The grizzly roared and started to attack, but Adams fixed his gaze on her eyes. She backed away, but kept up a long, deep growl.

"This little one is all right," Adams whispered, knowing that at any second the big bear could snap his neck with one swat, but the big bear just growled, swaying back and forth, staring at the bearded man's eyes.

"Go tend your wounds," he said, knowing that hurt bears would roll in the mud to balm their cuts and scrapes. He looked at her paw, figuring that the grizzly would never climb a tree again with two missing toes.

The big bear swatted out once, touching Adams' cheek, looked at her cub, then limped towards the woods, leaving her little one behind. At the edge of the clearing she turned, stood on her hind legs and let out an enormous roar that echoed through the mountains.

Claw held his face, trying to stop the bleeding. "How'd you do that?" he grunted, blinded in his left eye from the blood.

"Just meant her no harm," he said setting the cub down. The cub didn't follow its mother, staying right next to Adams, pulling at the fringe of his new buckskins.

Claw tried to focus but the pain was too intense. "Who are you?"

"Name's Adams," he said, stooping to check the vital signs of the two hunters. "You got two dead men here," he said.

Claw drew his pistol and pointed it wildly, unable to focus through the blood. "You won't be robbin' us."

"I'm no robber, and you're hunting on my land," Adams said, checking the dogs. They were dead also.

Even though Claw was in terrible pain, he had to laugh. "Your land? You're crazy. This is Digger Indian land. No white man lives out here."

"I do," Adams said, kneeling down to pick up the cub.

"That cub's mine," said Claw, getting to his feet.

Adams started to speak but heard the sound of approaching horses. A white man was leading a string of pack mules piled high with bear skins.

That was the other grizzlies I was smelling, Adams thought.

"You okay?" shouted the man leading the mules. His name was Trapper and he too wore heavy necklaces of bear teeth and claws. His cap was made from a bear's head.

"Bear got my face," Claw said, wincing at the pain.

Trapper nodded, the tic in his cheek pulling his facial muscles. "Got just 'bout everythin' else," he said, looking at the bodies. He was keeping a watch on Adams from the corner of his eye, trying to figure if the man with the old Kentucky rifle was friend or foe, trying to decide whether he'd have to kill him or not.

"And who be you?" Trapper finally asked.

Adams looked the man in the eye, figuring that here was a dangerous man. The cub struggled to get free but Adams held him tightly. "Name's Adams, James Capen Adams."

"He's a witch or somethin'," Claw shouted. He staggered over to the pack mules and pulled out a cloth to hold back the blood.

"Witch?" Trapper said. He looked at Adams. "That true that you're a wood spook?" But Adams didn't say a word.

Claw stepped forward with a bloody cloth held against his face. "Saw him put a hoodoo on that bear. Left her cub without a fight. No grizzly will do that."

Trapper's grin was evil. "That right?" he asked. "You know how to hoodoo a bear?" Trapper was just buying time until he had a bead on the man.

"Shoot him!" Claw shouted.

Adams shifted the cub to his left arm, pointing the Kentucky rifle at Trapper with the other. Trapper grinned, cool under pressure. "Shoot him? What for?" Trapper asked.

"'Cause he's got our cub," Claw said, wincing at the pain.

"That so?" Trapper asked, figuring the odds of getting his pistol out before the stranger could cock his rifle.

Adams looked at the pack mules. "You got enough skins there," he said. "Pack up and go."

"Only got ninety," Trapper shrugged.

"Ninety's more than enough," Adams frowned, disgusted by the slaughter.

"We want ninety-one," Trapper shrugged, looking at the cub.

Claw ran his tongue around his gums, holding his face together with his hand. "Trapper made a mistake. We want ninety-two."

Trapper gave a questioning look, so Claw said,

"Maybe we'll skin him; he looks like a grizzly himself." Trapper chuckled.

"I told you boys to go," Adams said, figuring he had a fight coming.

Claw walked up holding his pistol out. "We're not leavin' without the cub."

"That's right," Trapper grinned. "Either we kill the cub now, or we kill you first, then we kill the cub. Choice is yours seein' as you're outnumbered."

"What's your decision, stranger?" Claw hissed.

Without a second thought, Adams spun around, knocking the pistol out of Claw's hands with his rifle and shoving him backwards. Trapper's horse reared, coming down as Adams put his Kentucky rifle up against the other man's throat.

"Now here's your choice," Adams said slowly. The cub lay silently in his arm. "Either you both walk away now, or I'll shoot your trigger fingers off like you did that bear."

"You're bluffin'," Trapper said, his eyes ablaze.

"He's tryin' to hoodoo us like he did that bear," Claw muttered.

Adams didn't answer. He just counted silently, moving his lips. Trapper knew that this man before him was different. One who wouldn't back down.

Trapper looked at the two dead men, the dogs and Claw's ripped face. "Guess I might just enjoy a walk," he said, getting down from his horse.

Adams picked up Claw's pistol and tossed it over the cliff. "And what's your decision?" he asked the wounded man.

"He's walkin' with me," Trapper said, dismounting. He took Claw by the arm.

"You can't leave us without a gun or horse," Claw said. "We might not make it back."

"Take your horses," Adams said, "and your mules." Trapper's eyes brightened, thinking that they were going to get to keep the bearskins after all. But it was just a fleeting thought, because Adams continued, "But the bearskins stay."

"You must like grizzly bears an awful lot," Trapper said. "What you gonna do with these skins, trade 'em?"

"Bury 'em."

"Bury 'em?" Trapper exclaimed. "There's a fortune in skins there."

"Don't matter. Money doesn't mean anything to me anymore," Adams said.

"You must be crazy," Trapper said, looking Adams in the eyes.

"He's a witch," Claw said. "You should have seen the way he spelled that bear with his eyes." He mounted his horse and looked at Adams intensely through his one good eye. "What's your name, stranger?"

Adams hesitated. *Should I lie or tell him my real name?* He had nothing to hide, so he said, "I told you before, my name's Adams."

"I think he's part bear," Claw hissed.

Trapper looked at the bearskins they were leaving behind with this stranger. "Okay, Mr. Grizzly Adams, or whatever your name is. We're goin' now."

Claw dropped the bloody bandage and pointed his

finger at Adams. "Our paths will cross again, and only one of us will walk away."

Adams shook his head. "Don't ever come back to my mountain, or it'll be you that won't ever leave."

"Let's go," Trapper said, turning his horse.

"Take them with you," Adams said, pointing with his rifle to the two dead man.

Trapper loaded a body onto each horse, then kicked the sides of his mount. "See you again, Mr. Grizzly Adams," he chuckled.

Adams watched them ride away. On the far ridge he saw them dump the bodies of the two dead men over a ravine.

What have I gotten myself into? he wondered. *I've only been up here a month and already I've made enemies.*

From the top of the ridge he heard a bear roar and looked up. There above him was the big mother bear, standing upright, roaring at Adams. "I'll take good care of him," he whispered, squeezing the cub. The big bear disappeared into the woods.

The cub nipped at the fringe of his shirt. "Guess you're hungry," Grizzly smiled. He took the cub back to where the oxen were. Then he chopped up some jerky and the cub devoured it. Bandit watched, wondering what to make of this new housemate.

"What will I name you, little fella?" Adams laughed, as the cub tried to lick his face. Then he grinned. "There's only one human I still like. Ben Franklin. That's what I'm gonna call you." The cub squealed playfully, trying to nip at Adams' beard.

Before it was dark, Adams burned the bearskins in a bonfire and buried the ashes on the ridge where the hunters had left them. In the morning he would plant a pine tree on the spot to mark it. Freedom swooped down, flapped its wings over the grave, then circled twice and flew away.

From the woods, the Digger Indians watched, not sure what to make of this man who cuddled a grizzly bear cub. They also believed that there was something ghostly about the bear tracks they found around this mountain of a bear with the missing two toes. Within three years, James Capen Adams would become the stuff of legend. His exploits would be written about in newspapers and dime novels. His feats of daring would be whispered over campfires. He was a man who had power over animals, lived among the Indians, and stood his ground, yielding to no one.

He was the bravest mountain man of them all, and they called him Grizzly Adams.

CHAPTER THREE

Rendezvous

Six Years Later

Grizzly Adams leaned on his old Kentucky rifle watching the men below make fools of themselves. Some were dancing around with Indians, liquor bottles in their hands, shooting off guns and screaming out war cries.

"Darn fools," Grizzly said, shaking his head. His full-grown bear Ben Franklin sat by his side, watching the commotion.

Those who came to the rendezvous were mountain men. Most lived two days of paddling from the fringe of civilization and talked to no one for months on end. Fiercely independent, they chose the mountains, rivers, and hills over the settlers' towns.

They were hunters and trappers, like the other rugged men of all colors who lived off the land. Some were running from the law and some were running from lost loves, but they all seemed to be running from something, and Grizzly Adams was no exception.

Dressed in patched buckskins, wearing tough, rawhide-soled moccasins, they had traded civilization for the mountains and beaver streams. They'd chosen the cottonwood, willow, aspen and birch instead of forts and settlements; cabins and Indian lodges over churches and trade stores. They had chosen to live their lives their own way, do or die.

Various tribes had traveled to the rendezvous to trade and drink. Grizzly Adams knew that you could never be friends with all the Indians, just like you could never like or be liked by all the settlers coming West. With over a million Indians in the western states broken down into at least six hundred distinct societies with two hundred and fifty different languages, Grizzly had done his best to learn about the Indians whose boundaries touched his mountain territory.

He'd stopped by the annual rendezvous on his way back from hunting game for the Digger Indians, whose land he shared. The fringes of his pants and sleeves were in tatters, there were empty gaps where he'd pulled off pieces of buckskin to mend his moccasins and pack saddles. More than six months had passed since he'd last been to Fort Henderson to get supplies, which was still a day's canoe ride away.

He had been in the wilderness only six years but looked like he'd been there all his life. Adams wasn't a big man, but his wiry, muscular frame let you know he was not one to be challenged easily. His body bore the scars of fights with men and beasts that would have left a weaker man dead long ago.

With a heavy beard, mustache, and long hair which hung over his shoulders, he looked like he'd been born in the mountains, not outside of Boston. He wore his hair long to protect his eyes, ears and neck and in many ways to measure time.

He trimmed it just twice a year, when he went down to Fort Henderson.

His face was deeply tanned, contrasting against the beaded Indian choker that the Diggers had made for him. It was a small gesture to thank Grizzly Adams for the laudanum he'd bought for them to help against the outbreak of cholera introduced to the mountains by settlers. The other beadwork on his shirt and coat were from different tribes, showing that he traded with them.

There were less people at the rendezvous than usual, which Adams figured was due to the deadly spread of cholera and smallpox. They were brought West with the wagon trains and East from the rats on the ships on the California coast. No place was safe, not even Grizzly Adams' mountains.

On the other side of the dancing, an intense game of Ferret Legging was going on. The weasel-like ferrets were used by the mountain men to hunt rabbits, and at the rendezvous, they were part of a very painful game.

The game was simple. Each mountain man who dared to enter tied up the bottom of his pants legs, dropped a ferret down each leg, then stood there as the animals bit and scratched as they fought to escape. The winner was the man who stood the pain and was the last to drop his britches.

Grizzly laughed, looking at the tough mountain men trying not to scream. "Wouldn't catch me doin' that, Ben," he said to the big grizzly bear he'd saved six years before.

Betting was intense as the trappers laid down gold or trade muskets on which man would drop his pants first. As one man after another dropped their drawers, crying out to get the ferrets off their bloody legs, Grizzly watched as it came down to a tall Crow Indian and a black mountain man with an unusually long knife strapped to his buckskinned leg. Grizzly had heard of a black mountain man who carried a knife that size and figured him to be the one they called Longknife.

"Gonna have two legless fools," Grizzly said, wondering how either of them could stand the pain of the ferrets biting and scraping at their legs.

The Indian was a tall handsome man, far bigger than the others. His face was pockmarked, evidence that he'd survived smallpox. He wore a necklace of animal teeth, and his hair was cut to the pattern of his tribe, with long strands taken from those he'd killed woven on the sides until it touched the ground. Grizzly knew it was the Crow's way of bragging, of daring his enemies to come try to scalp him.

The black mountain man called Longknife began singing out a rowdy verse of "Yankee Doodle," dancing around like he was at a picnic.

"Somethin' botherin' you, chief?" he joked, seeing the bloody buckskins on the Indian's legs.

The mountain men made a ring around them, wondering how Longknife could be so calm. Most had tried the game once and had the scars to prove why they'd never try it again.

"Hey, chief," Longknife said, dancing around, "you like my song?" he laughed, singing another bawdy verse. The Indian just glared.

Finally, after the Indian's buckskins were soaked red with blood, the ferrets ate their way out of his pants. Longknife grinned. "Guess you lose, chief."

The Indian's eyes flared, looking at the ferret lumps in the man's pants which seemed hardly to be moving. "You cheated," he said, "those ferrets are dead."

The black mountain man smiled, "Wrong again, chief," he said. "Longknife's just smarter than you," he laughed, dropping his pants. He was wearing another set of buckskins underneath. The two ferrets rolled out and lay on the ground, like they were in a daze.

The Crow knelt down painfully on his bloody leg, looking at the animals. He picked one up and sniffed it. "Whiskey!" he grunted.

Longknife burst out laughing. "Only a damned fool would drop skin-eatin' animals down their drawers. Guess you boys are all fools," he said, looking at the other mountain men who'd entered and lost and were now wiping the blood from their legs.

"Pay up, boys," Longknife said, pulling up his britches. He put the two ferrets in a sack on his back, then went around to collect his winnings.

A moment of tension passed before all the mountain men burst out laughing. The Crow Indian stood up and looked the black man in the eye. The crowd tensed as Longknife moved his hand toward his big knife.

Before the Crow could draw his blade, Longknife pulled out his twenty-inch knife and threw it towards the Indian. The Crow froze as the knife landed between his legs.

Longknife walked over and yanked it from the ground. "Next time, it won't be the ferret that will be takin' your jewels," he whispered, winking at the Indian.

The Indian took a breath, then grinned. "Nice scalp," he grunted, "I've never taken a black man's scalp."

"And you won't be startin' with mine," Longknife

said, holding out his knife. The Indian glared and turned and walked away through the chuckling crowd.

"Now I'll go check out the women those braves got to trade," Longknife chuckled, nodding to the trappers around him. He walked through the crowd singing "Yankee Doodle."

Grizzly smiled. "Drunken ferrets. That man's got smarts and guts." Ben growled playfully, pulling at the fringe on Grizzly's leggings.

"In a little while. First I want to go down and see who made it through the year," he said to Ben, thinking about those he'd already buried from the diseases that had wiped out whole mountain towns.

Grizzly picked up his rifle and walked toward the tents below. "Stay, Ben," he commanded. "I won't be long." The big grizzly bear sat down, watching Adams walk down the short slope.

"Hey, Grizzly Adams, didn't 'spect to see you at the rendezvous," an old mountain man, nicknamed Flash-in-the-Pan for his flintlock's misfires, called out from a tent.

Grizzly looked, trying to see who called his name, but there was so much drunken ruckus going on that it was hard to hear anything. Flash stepped out and grinned a toothless smile. "Thought you'd given up these things."

"Was just on my path home," Adams nodded. "Good to see you, Flash," he said, putting his arm around the old hunter. "You doin' all right?" he asked, seeing the smallpox marks on the man's face.

"So-so," the old man shrugged. "If I can survive

smallpox, I can survive old age."

"You're one of the lucky ones."

"'Bout wiped out them trappers huntin' for the English up in the Nevadas," Flash confided.

A gambler in a tall beaver hat nodded to Adams. "You still eyein' down bears?" he chuckled.

"Easier than eyein' down a card sharpie like you."

"Hey, Adams," called out another, "you want yourself a fat wife?" Grizzly Adams shook his head and the man laughed. "She'll keep you warm in the winter."

"My bear keeps me warm enough," Grizzly said, jokingly.

Flash looked around. "Where's your bear, anyway?"

Adams shouted out, "Ben, here!" Several Indian women screamed as the big bear come loping out of the woods.

A few of the drunken mountain men who'd never seen Grizzly Adams or his bear grabbed their rifles. "Don't shoot," Adams said. "He's my bear."

Ben Franklin came up to Grizzly and put his paws up. "Down, Ben," he laughed.

"Guess you won't need a wife if you got her," Flash laughed.

"Him, not a her. Name's Ben, Ben Franklin," Grizzly said, walking through the crowd that parted before him.

"Hey, Grizzly," Flash called out, "heard 'bout a man swearin' he was going to kill you." But the noise was too loud and Adams didn't hear him.

CHAPTER FOUR

Longknife

Once the Hudson Bay Company had shipped more than a million beaver pelts to Europe to make ten-dollar fashionable hats, the beaver trade ended. With the beaver all but extinct, the mountain men were left to hunt for coat fur, which didn't bring nearly the same price.

With the high-dollar beaver trade finished, the rendezvous had turned into nothing more than a drunken get-together by the 1850s. Men who hid from civilization for eleven months of the year would travel for days to spend several weeks, lounging around, gambling, and swapping stories.

It was a chance to stock up on supplies, learn who'd lived and died the previous year and re-equip for the coming year. Indians came to swap furs for trinkets, weapons, and gunpowder and enjoy the rowdy feasts.

It was also a time for Indian women to be traded and wives bought, which was what Longknife was now trying to do. Grizzly stopped to watch the haggling, amused at the way Longknife was outtalking the Crow Indians in their own language.

"Look, chief," Longknife said. He called every Indian that. "I'm half horse and half alligator, with a little touch of snapping turtle mixed with the silky stomach of a beaver. I've got a wildcat in each hand, and if that don't make me man enough for one of your women, nothin' will."

Grizzly grinned, watching the Indian try to translate that to the others. He turned to see Flash standing beside him. "What are Crows doin' in these parts anyway?" he asked the old man.

"Them Crows are the ones that moved in on the Yosemites' land tryin' to escape the cholera."

Grizzly paused, puzzled at the old man's reticence. "What else?" he asked.

The old man hesitated. Then he spoke. "They're huntin' bear for a medicine man named Bear Robe who says that bear teeth and claws can ward off the sickness."

Grizzly listened, feeling sorry for the Indians. He knew that the diseases were virtually uncontainable once they broke out. He'd heard that they had already ravaged the Mississippi Valley. St. Louis had lost a tenth of its population. Cincinnati the same. Half the Eighth Regiment of the US Army had died in Texas. A million whites and Indians had been left with pockmarked faces, the scars of survivors.

The mountain trails were filled with crosses and stone cairns where pioneers had buried their kin where they dropped. Many of the large wagon trains coming West had lost two thirds of their members and there were huge numbers of orphans being sent West from ravaged East-coast cities like Boston.

Flash coughed. "Bear Robe's got a bunch of renegades with him. Bad bunch." Flash looked at Adams. "I think they're the ones been killin' the settlers that the cholera ain't got."

Grizzly had heard about settlers' cabins being burned, but thought it was a roving band of Paiutes from the Nevadas who were responsible. It was also one of the ways the disease was moving so fast through the plains and mountains, because the Indians would rob the clothes from the graves of cholera and smallpox victims, not knowing that the diseases were spread that way.

Grizzly considered Flash's words. "What makes you think these Indians are doin' it?" he asked, eyeing the Crows.

He saw the scalps the moment Flash nodded toward them. "I know you saw 'em. Damned Indians are walkin' 'round proud of their trophies." The old man shook his head and spat in disgust. It was the unwritten rule of the rendezvous that old fights were left aside during the party time.

"Can't stop the Indians from killin' each other," Grizzly said.

"Them's not all Indian scalps," Flash whispered. "Unless you know of some blond and red-headed Indians that I ain't never heard of." Hanging from the Crow's horses and belts were scalps of various colors.

"Who's the big Indian?" Grizzly asked, nodding toward the one that Longknife had beaten in the ferret legging contest. He had never seen an Indian with hair that hung so far down.

Flash shrugged. "Calls himself Thundercloud or Thunder Over the Mountains, or Thunder in His Pants. Heck, I never can remember all them silly Indian names. Everyone just calls him Thunder."

Flash paused then said, "Got somethin' else you ought to know."

Before Grizzly could answer, he sensed something

was wrong. He looked over and saw that Thunder was now moving toward where Longknife was haggling over the Crow woman he wanted for a wife.

"Trouble's 'bout to happen," Flash whispered. Others noticed too and moved back to give the Indian room.

As Thunder drew his blade, Grizzly stepped forward, drawing his own knife. "Don't," he said, looking the Crow in the eye.

"Stay out of it, Adams," someone shouted.

Longknife turned. "You want somethin', chief?" Several of the white mountain men gathered around.

"Let them fight it out," a burly red-headed mountain man jeered.

"Yeah," said a man that Grizzly Adams thought he recognized, "that black son'bitch cheated Thunder." It was Trapper, wearing a new bear-head hat.

Longknife looked between them, quickly sizing up that Grizzly Adams was the only one who was standing with him. "Didn't cheat, just joked, that's all."

"Men don't think that's funny," Trapper said. "Wearin' two sets o' britches and usin' drunken ferrets."

Longknife opened up his sack and held up the ferrets. "These are Yankee and Doodle, like the song, "Yankee Doodle." He started humming the song, trying to break the tension in the air, but it didn't do any good. The ferrets slowly twitched their feet like they were waking up.

Trapper shook his head. "Men 'round here don't like you usin' drunken ferrets."

Longknife tried to think fast. "What's wrong with a little drink now and then? Why, Yankee, Doodle, and I do everythin' together."

The big red-headed mountain man jeered, "Maybe they want to get buried together. What do you think, Trapper?"

The mountain men heard Trapper's name and moved back. Trapper took off the bear-head cap and scratched the hair that remained. Partially scalped in an Indian fight two years before, he was half-crazy and loved killing. Men at the rendezvous had heard the whispers that Trapper had "broken brains."

Grizzly cleared his throat. "Okay, boys, it's all over. Joke's a joke."

"Stay out of it, Adams," Trapper said, the tic beneath his eye beginning to twitch.

Grizzly stared, trying to place him. "Do I know you, stranger?"

"Our paths crossed years before."

"Don't recognize the scar," Grizzly said.

Trapper put his cap back on. "It happened after we had us our little run-in." It came back to Grizzly; Trapper could see it in his eyes. "Good to see you, Adams. You still got our bear pelts?"

"Told you to not come back," Grizzly said quietly.

"You don't own the whole world," Trapper laughed. "You still got our bear cub?"

"Ben, now!" Grizzly snapped, and his big grizzly bear came up by his side, growling at Trapper.

Trapper was not one to be scared easily. "Got no fight with you, Adams, or your bear." He looked at the

Indian. "Come on, Thunder, let's go."

Grizzly Adams watched the two men walk away. Behind them followed the band of Crow Indians and the women they'd brought to barter and sell.

Longknife grinned and stuck out his hand. "Guess I owe you, Adams. Name's Longknife."

"I've heard 'bout you," Grizzly said.

"And I've heard 'bout you. Saw someone in my last run through Sacramento who had a picture book 'bout you." Longknife whistled. "Imagine that, havin' a story writ all 'bout you," he said, putting the ferrets back in his sack.

"I've seen it," Grizzly said, too modest to brag about the dime novel that had been written about him.

Longknife looked in the direction the Crows had gone. "Sure could have used one of them Indian woman for the winter. I've been lonely so long that I've been flirtin' with myself," he said, then burst out laughing at his own joke.

"You got yourself an Indian wife?" Longknife asked.

"No, I live alone and like it that way," Grizzly said.

"You should get yourself some female company. Keep you warm when it snows."

"Good luck to you, Longknife," Grizzly said, turning to go. Behind him stood Flash, who cleared his throat.

"That's the other thing I was tryin' to tell you." Grizzly turned to find Flash nodding. "Trapper and a man named Claw Wyler came through the rendezvous, leadin' a bunch of renegades and Crows that Thunder's ridin' with. Said he was lookin' for you."

"For me? What'd he look like?"

Flash closed his eyes. "Half his face was about pulled off. Worse thing I ever saw. Like he was a walkin' dead man or somethin'."

The old man watched the reaction on Grizzly's face, then said, "He said he's lookin' to kill you and your bear and a big bear that's missing two toes."

"I heard 'bout that ghost bear," Longknife said. "Supposed to be 'bout as big as a beer wagon."

Flash coughed again. "Said he'd pay a hundret dollars to the man who killed that bear and brought it in."

Longknife whistled. "Whooee, maybe I should just go bear huntin'."

"Leave the big bear alone," Grizzly said sternly. He looked Longknife in the eyes, then looked at Flash. "Thanks for the warning," Grizzly said. "Ben, move," he ordered, and the grizzly moved out alongside him.

"Hey, Griz, what way you headed?" Longknife called out.

"My own way," Grizzly said, walking off.

"I was headin' just that way myself," Longknife said, wanting to put distance between the Crows and himself. He followed after Grizzly Adams whistling "Yankee Doodle."

Grizzly looked back. "Why don't you go home or somethin'. Leave me alone."

Longknife frowned. "Was a slave back in Georgia and I don't think I could get back to Africa, so I came West, which is your lucky day."

"Some luck," Grizzly groaned.

"Want to know how I got out here and become a mountain man?"

"No," Grizzly grunted. "Go tell someone else."

"Well, sir," Longknife said, taking a breath to say his brag. "I came West riding a mountain lion, whipping him over the head with a pistol, pickin' my teeth with a Kentucky rifle, wearing two Bowie knives which I had made into one and using a cactus to comb my hair. Nobody messes with ol' Longknife."

"Except those Crows back there," Grizzly grinned, amused by the man's bragging but not wanting to show it.

"I was just waitin' them out. Wanted to let them make their move 'fore I stepped out," Longknife said. "What 'bout you? Where you from?"

Grizzly didn't say anything so Longknife just rattled on. "From the looks of you, I bet that you were raised in the backwoods, probably suckled by a cinnamon bear and got barbed wire intestines from the raw animals you eat."

"Probably so," Grizzly said. He stayed silent until he cleared the rendezvous, figuring that Longknife would go away, but the man kept following. Longknife called out, "Don't you like to talk, or's that grizzly got your tongue?"

Grizzly shook his head. "Come on, Ben, just ignore him."

Longknife shrugged, then laughed, thinking about the ferret legging game. "Yes, sir, man's the only animal that can be skinned more'n once and I bet I've skinned those ol' boys 'bout a hundret times."

But Adams didn't say a thing. Finally, Longknife ran up beside him and asked, "Your mouth broke or somethin'?"

Grizzly stopped and looked at the man who wouldn't stop following him. "The bigger the mouth, the better it looks shut, which is how I'd like to see yours."

"So you do talk," Longknife nodded. "Can't a man just thank you for savin' his life?"

"I accept your thanks and now I'd be grateful if you'd just go on back to the rendezvous and leave me alone."

"You want to know where I learned that trick puttin' Yankee and Doodle down my britches?"

"I wouldn't care if Yankee bit your whatever. Serve you right gettin' ferrets drunked up." Grizzly looked at his bear. "Ben, move."

"There you go again," Longknife said, running to catch up. "'Ben, move.' That all you got to say when I'm offerin' you my friendship for savin' my life?"

"I ain't lookin' for friends. I want to be left alone," Grizzly said. Ben growled his agreement.

"Then how 'bout a travelin' companion?"

"Got one," Grizzly said, nodding to his bear.

"But a bear don't talk," Longknife said in frustration.

"That's why I like him," Grizzly said.

"Just tell me where you're from," Longknife said, acting as if he was going to turn and leave.

Grizzly coughed. "I'm from Massachusetts."

"Mass-ass-chu-sets?" Longknife laughed. "The shoemaker state?"

"That I was," Grizzly nodded, not wanting to think about the past.

"No!"

"Yes, now leave me be and go away," Grizzly said.

"But we could be neighbors," Longknife replied, "good neighbors. Kind who could help each other out and..."

Grizzly stopped and held up his hand. "Look, stranger, I stood with you and you thanked me, now you don't owe me a thing." Longknife started to speak but Grizzly held up his finger for quiet. "I don't need friends or traveling companions, and I don't need neighbors."

He turned abruptly and said over his shoulder, "So you go your way and I'll go mine."

"And wherever our paths cross that will be okay?" Longknife called out.

"It'll be okay," Grizzly said, not knowing what Longknife had in mind.

The mountain man took out his ferrets and smiled. "Guess we're goin' to just follow behind Mr. Grizzly up there and see where our paths cross." He put the ferrets back in his sack and started out after Grizzly. "Yes, sir, I bet our paths will cross 'bout where his cabin is or wherever a man with a bear lives."

He walked a few steps forward then shivered. "Hope he don't live in no cave. I sure don't need that kind of friend." Then he smiled and began singing "Yankee Doodle" again.

Up ahead, Grizzly Adams winced at the sound. "Ben, these woods are gettin' too crowded."

"Say, Griz, how'd you get the name Grizzly Adams anyway?" Longknife called. "That your birth name?"

But Grizzly didn't answer. He just walked ahead,

hoping to put a lot of distance between himself and this talkative mountain man.

CHAPTER FIVE

Claw Wyler

Claw Wyler looked at Trapper. It had taken Trapper and the Crows a day longer to get back from the rendezvous and he was furious. "And you're sure it was him?"

Trapper fluttered his lips. The tic in his cheek twitched because he was under pressure. "How many men you know walk 'round with grizzly bears?" Trapper didn't like being questioned.

"And he's still back where he bushwhacked us?" Though it had been six years, Claw had relived the encounter a thousand times in his mind.

Trapper shrugged. "Heard he's built hisself a cabin and settled right in."

Claw itched at the thick scars that lined the left side of his face. It looked like the skin had melted, ready to slide off his face at any second. His eye drooped and he was virtually blind in that one eye.

"Then we're goin' back that way," Claw said. "I got a score to settle."

Trapper shook his head, looking over at the Crows who were talking with Bridger, the other white man in the group. "Don't think that's so good an idea," he said. "We got almost 'nough bearskins and claws for the medicine man. Don't need to go lookin' for a fight."

The renegades who followed Claw Wyler were a motley bunch, dressed in dirty skins and furs. The Indians in the band wore split feathers, signifying that they had cut the throats and taken the scalps of many enemies.

The three Crow Indians were striking men, with hair parted on each side. The hair over their foreheads stood upright and over the temples it was cut in a zig-zag pattern. Colorful braids held the long side locks together.

The jewelry the Crows wore was from the settlers they'd killed. Square-cut scalps hung at their belts, some braided, some straight, depending on whether they were from Indians or whites. It was one of the benefits of hunting with Claw Wyler, a man who turned on his own kind.

Each of the renegades wore necklaces of bear claws and teeth, their share of the hunt to use to trade for women and goods. They'd left two other Crow Indians at their hunting camp to guard the horses, packmules and the bearskins they'd already taken.

Since July, they'd combed the Sierras, killing scores of bears in a trade deal with the Crow medicine man, Bear Robe. It was an unholy alliance born of greed and revenge.

Teeth, claws, hides and bear cubs were swapped for the pick of the settlers' belongings that Bear Robe's men had taken in their raids on the isolated cabins. Bear Robe was trying to keep the diseases from killing off what was left of his tribe, as they had done to the other Indians back in their old land.

Bear Robe had brought his small tribe from the Northern territories, through Commanche, Shoshoni and Paiute lands, to fulfill the vision of the bears he'd had. The vision of the power of the teeth and claws to ward off the white man's diseases which had run through their tribe faster than an enemy's lance.

The small band of Crows that hadn't succumbed to the diseases followed his vision, pushing out the Mariposa and Yosemite tribes in the Sierras who got in their way. They were pockmarked warriors, with horribly scarred faces, willing to do anything to stop the diseases.

Though there were plenty of black and cinnamon bears, Bear Robe wanted grizzlies, believing their medicine the strongest. He thought the black bear too common and small and since it avoided man, he considered it cowardly. The cinnamon bears were small, like the black bears, and were relatively harmless if left alone. Bear Robe had never seen one measure more than five feet, and again thought they were not worthy because they usually ran when challenged.

But the grizzly was a worthy opponent and possessed the strong medicine he needed to fight the deadly diseases. Bear Robe had seen grizzlies over ten feet tall, weighing two thousand pounds. With a dirty brown or grizzly gray coat, and eight-inch claws which could kill a buffalo or a horse with one blow, they were the most powerful animals in the wilderness.

But what drove Claw to kill bears was not the goods or women. This vicious man was driven by revenge. Bear Robe had promised to show him where the great ghost bear with the two missing toes lived. It was the bear that had ripped Claw's face and he'd dreamed of killing it in revenge.

But he also wanted to kill the man called Grizzly

Adams and the bear cub he'd kept from them. Claw looked in the direction where he figured Grizzly Adams' mountain was, focusing his good eye. Trapper watched, knowing to not interfere when Claw started mumbling to himself.

"I vowed I'd come back to kill you, Grizzly Adams, and kill that bear of yours and the big gray one for what she done to my face."

Trapper couldn't help but add his piece. "You'll never find it."

"I'll find her," Claw growled. "She's the only bear who leaves tracks with two missing toes."

He'd seen the tracks twice since the encounter with the big gray, but had never gotten close to it.

"These mountains all look alike," Trapper shrugged. "Not like the ones we been huntin' in up in the Oregons. That bear could be anywhere."

"I said we'll find her," Claw said, walking to the edge of the cliff.

"Did I tell you 'bout the sweet little cabin we done found 'bout a mile back?" Trapper asked, a twinkle in his eye.

Claw cocked his head. "Any children?"

Trapper chuckled. "Couple. I figured that since we're short a few skins, why, we might just make up for it with more kids."

They'd already burned down a dozen cabins within a week's walk in all directions, but in the isolated mountains, only the ones they'd destroyed near Fort Henderson were known.

"Come on, Claw, let's go check out that cabin 'fore it

gets dark," Trapper called out. He had the glint in his eye of a man who lusted for the kill.

"You tell Thunder that they're not to kill the children this time."

Trapper laughed, shaking his head. "Two out of ten ain't bad. You got to admit that."

Claw shrugged. Bear Robe had asked for more children after they'd brought in the last bunch they'd kidnapped, to trade them to the Snake River Indians for more bear teeth.

"You just tell them to take the scalps but leave the kids," Claw said.

"What 'bout women?" Trapper winked.

"What 'bout 'em?" Claw asked, knowing full well what Trapper meant.

"Just that I'm lonely and..."

Claw stopped him short. "You're already a squaw man," Claw said, knowing that Trapper had two Indian wives in the Oregons.

"Can always use more," he smiled. "Heck, Bear Robe's got ten."

Claw was in no mood to joke. "There's not much time left to finish our hunt. We'll trade what we find to Bear Robe."

Trapper shook his head and spit. "That medicine man ain't never gonna help you find that ghost bear you're wantin'. Me, why, I'd just stop thinkin' 'bout it."

"Don't you still think 'bout the Indian who scalped you?" Claw asked. "Don't you want revenge?"

Trapper shrugged. "I killed a couple injuns that

looked like him, so I figured I 'bout evened the score."
He walked off to where Bridger and the others were
standing.

Claw turned back towards the mountains. "I told you
I'd come back, Grizzly Adams," he whispered. He
could taste the blood of revenge on his lips. He'd waited a long time to come back, and wouldn't leave until
either he or Grizzly Adams was dead.

But first he had to find the tracks of the ghost bear.

CHAPTER SIX

Neighbors

Grizzly Adams looked out over his mountain valley, listening to the wind. He'd counted thirty graves, cholera victims, on the trail back from the rendezvous and saw a dozen boarded-up cabins.

With the sickness to worry about and Claw Wyler threatening to kill him, Grizzly had a lot on his mind. He was also not used to having company but the man called Longknife had followed him. It was bad enough that he'd been talked into telling him the story about Claw Wyler and Ben Franklin, but the man kept wanting to know more.

Can't understand why he won't take the hints and leave, Grizzly frowned. Bandit came out and sat beside him but Grizzly barely noticed.

I hate his singin'. Always singin' that "Yankee Doodle" *song or talkin' to his ferrets. Man's got a mouth bigger than the Mississippi.*

He'd done all he could to get the man to go, even telling him bluntly that it was time to leave. Grizzly thought Longknife had gotten the message when he'd packed up and left for the night, but he'd come back the next morning, saying he'd built a lodge on the other side of the mountain and that they were now neighbors.

Neighbors, Grizzly thought, shaking his head. *I came out to the wilderness to escape people and in moves a neighbor. And a big-mouth one at that.*

Besides the Digger Indians, the only other white man who lived in his woods was a crazy old man named Peepers, who lived in a cave somewhere in the valley.

He had long, tangled gray hair, sunken eyes and the kind of look that made the Indians believe he was an evil spirit. *If this Longknife was like Peepers it wouldn't be so bad. Peepers's just crazy and leaves me presents. Don't bother me none at all.* Grizzly frowned. *And he don't sing that song over and over. I'm gettin' to hate that* "Yankee Doodle" *song.*

Grizzly had tried to find where Peepers lived, but the man just seemed to vanish. *But he watches me, that I know,* Grizzly thought.

And now he had to go to Fort Henderson and restock for the winter. *Can't put it off any longer*, he sighed, wondering what the people of the town would think when he showed up this year with his bear and another mountain man who told everyone that they were neighbors.

He sighed, wishing that he'd never stopped by the rendezvous in the first place. *Maybe I can just sneak off without him*, he thought, but he knew that Longknife had been talking nonstop about going to the fort with him.

I'm trapped, he frowned. *Like a city rat. I'm trapped with a neighbor I didn't ask for, want, or need.*

As was his custom, Adams had put off going to Fort Henderson until the snows were almost upon him. He'd seen the animals preparing for winter. Chipmunks and squirrels were foraging. Badgers, bears, and raccoons were eating heavily, preparing to lower their body temperatures. Grizzly had even seen the few bats that hibernated flying in feeding frenzies on the night wind.

"But none of them got neighbors like Longknife," he grumbled. Grizzly wasn't used to having a man hanging around his cabin singing songs, telling jokes, and asking questions. *Man asks more questions than I've been asked in a lifetime*, Grizzly thought, shaking his head. *And half the time he don't even go back to his lodge, just rolls out his blanket and sleeps on my floor like he owned the place.*

Freedom swooped down and landed on the stump. He flapped his wings, dancing around like he was trying to tell Grizzly something. "What is it, Freedom?" Grizzly asked. Bandit scampered under the cabin, worried that the eagle would eat him.

Grizzly looked in the eagle's eyes, then nodded. "You've seen trouble, haven't ya?" The eagle cawed then flew away toward the west.

It made Grizzly think about Trapper and the man named Claw Wyler. *I can feel that man comin' after me*, he thought, thinking about the run-in he'd had when he first came to the Sierras. *Said he'd come back to kill me and Ben.*

Behind him, the simple cabin contained everything Adams owned in the world. Simple things, handmade things, the necessities of life. He was rich in ways that most men would never understand, counting the wilderness, the mountains, and his animals as his real treasures in life. But it wasn't to get rich that he'd become a mountain man. He'd fled the East to find freedom, to find himself.

Taking a deep breath, Grizzly Adams smelled the soul of his beloved mountains. *Got to be a way to work through this*, he thought, believing that with his new neighbor and Claw Wyler, he needed some higher power to help. Though he wasn't a churchgoing man, Grizzly Adams had his own prayers and found God's grandeur in the wilderness around him.

Touching the pine that grew on the ridge where he'd buried the bear skins, Grizzly breathed in his mountains, taking them into his heart. *You can still find God's path in a pathless forest*, he thought, watching the eagle take flight from the top of the tall pine. *There's no loneliness in the lonely woods*, he nodded, then frowned.

"Especially with Longknife movin' hisself in," Grizzly groaned.

Ben Franklin nuzzled against his leg, pawing at the ground. Grizzly reached down and scratched the animal's big head.

Against the door of the cabin behind him were his Kentucky and Tennessee rifles. A bone-handled knife hung from his waist, strapped to the thick, leather Colt revolver belt. He went everywhere armed, worried more about dangerous men than animals.

From a shoemaker to a mountain man, it's been a long way to come, Grizzly thought. *I'm a couple hundred days ride from Massachusetts, but it doesn't seem far enough...'specially now that I've got me a neighbor. If I have to hear the story 'bout that big knife of his one more time, I'll go crazy.*

"Why'd I go to the durn rendezvous in the first place!" he grumbled, unconsciously fingering the grease spot on his buckskin sleeve. Ben Franklin nipped playfully at his fingers.

"Talkin' to yourself again?" asked Longknife who walked up from behind him. Yankee and Doodle were peeking out from his carry-sack.

"Thought you were gone for the day," Grizzly said, breathing deeply to bring himself under control. Ben sat up, pawing playfully at the air.

"Best you don't be lettin' anyone else hear you talk your mind out loud. Some folks might think you're crazy," smiled Longknife. Then he looked at Ben. "Course anyone who keeps a bear for a pet *is* crazy."

"Guess if I was you I'd move further away then. No sense livin' too close to a crazy man," Grizzly said, a slight grin breaking the deep wrinkles around his lips. No matter how hard he tried, he couldn't dislike the man. It was just that he wasn't used to company and hadn't sought it.

"Thought I saw a big gray bear off in the distance this mornin'," Longknife said.

"Where?" Grizzly asked. He'd felt something, a strange sensation, like he was being watched. Ben had been acting funny too.

"Over down towards the Diggers' camp."

"What were you doin' down there?" Grizzly asked. "You ain't gonna try that ferret leggin' game on them, are you?"

Longknife looked offended. "Me? No sir! I say you never fool your neighbors or in-laws."

There was something in the way the man said in-laws that worried Grizzly. "What were you exactly doin' down there?"

Longknife shrugged. "Winter's comin' on and I was lookin' for a wife." Then he closed his eyes and made a face. "Some of them are sooooo ugly."

Grizzly had to laugh. "Look who's talkin'," he grinned.

Longknife chuckled. "But there's a couple of fat ones down there be better'n ten blankets in the winter. Got my eye on two chubby sisters who can cook pretty good. I call them my sweet little Buffalo Girls."

"Why don't you just move down there with them squaws?" Grizzly asked.

"'Cause I'm your neighbor and I kind of like it here," Longknife shrugged. He looked at Grizzly. "You ever think 'bout marryin' one of them Digger squaws? Way they think 'bout you, why, you could have yourself the pick o' the litter. Might even make you a chief or somethin'."

"'Preciate the compliment but I don't need a woman none, thank you."

Longknife shook his head. "You been livin' with that stinky-breath bear too long. You need to get yourself to town sometime, and dance, meet you a woman, have you a pack of kids." Then Longknife laughed heartily. "'Course I can't 'magine you dancin'." He looked at Grizzly's big feet. "Bet you'd step all over the ladies' toes."

Grizzly looked away, wishing that he could just be alone. *Dancin'...pack of kids,* he thought shaking his head, *that's just what I don't need.*

"That's right," Longknife said, "it could be Papa Grizzly and his little bears. Mama bear could be fixin' me up a mess of grub right now and..."

Grizzly gave him a stern look. "Can't you just be quiet for a second?"

Longknife stood patiently, waiting for his newfound friend to get in a better mood. Grizzly turned away, deep in thought. Leaning against his .50 caliber Hawken half-stock flintlock rifle, Longknife had stopped trying to get this man who lived with animals to talk when he wasn't ready.

"You want me to sing a couple songs for you?" Longknife grinned, knowing that his singing bothered the mountain man.

"None today, thank you," Grizzly said.

Longknife chuckled. The sun's rays reflected off his handsome, ebony face. This grandson of an African warrior, who carried a hunter's blood in his veins, had taken an instant liking to this loner.

He thought about returning to the Indian-style lodge he'd put up on the other side of the mountain but decided to wait.

"You 'bout ready for some food?" Longknife asked, but Grizzly didn't answer. Longknife watched the bearded man stare out toward the mountains. *Wish I could get him to talk more. Make him laugh even. He's been livin' up here too long.*

Longknife figured that Grizzly Adams had saved his life and he owed him. And if the mountain man wasn't ready to accept that fact, then Longknife was ready to wait him out. *If it hadn't been for Griz, my scalp would have been hangin' on a Crow's lodge pole*, he thought.

Though Longknife liked to joke, he also had a serious side from suffering through being born into slavery. But he'd escaped and headed first North than West, trying to find freedom. Finally, he'd headed into the wilderness.

So when Grizzly had stood up for him, it did something to him. It was one of those moments that define a man, and from that moment on, Longknife knew the measure of Grizzly Adams. Not afraid to stand his ground, not afraid to do what was right, and not afraid of standing with a black man against his own color.

It was also a moment that Longknife knew that color still counted, even out in the wilderness. No matter how far he'd tried to get away from the slave states, the barriers never seemed to fall. And now with the trouble brewing in the East between the abolitionists and the slavers, he wondered if there was any place on Earth where he'd be truly free.

What ate at him were the whites that had turned against him without warning at the rendezvous. Men he'd hunted, trapped, and traveled with. Men he'd called friends, believing that the woods and trails had bonded them together.

Thought I had a lot of friends up here, friends that I could count on. But now I can count all my real friends on one hand with four fingers left over.

Longknife looked over again at the loner whom he now called a friend. Grizzly Adams just stared at the distant mountain tops, deep in thought, deep in his own world. Longknife reached inside his colorful, beaded full-length coat, looking for kinikinik. But the tobacco was gone, as were most of his supplies.

"What say we go down to Fort Henderson and stock ourselves up for the winter, neighbor?" Longknife asked, but Grizzly shook his head.

"Not ready," Grizzly grunted, "and don't call me neighbor."

"But that's what we are," Longknife responded.

"You're just vistin'."

Longknife shrugged and grinned. "Could be a lifetime visit so you best get used to it."

Grizzly closed his eyes and grimaced at the thought.

Longknife ignored him. "You could sure use a haircut, you know that," he said, looking at Grizzly's shaggy locks. "You afraid of gettin' your hair cut?" Longknife teased.

"I've looked death in the eye, so trimmin' my locks don't worry me none," Grizzly said, as if that said it all.

"Thought you might want one of the Buffalo Girls so we could be in-laws," Longknife said. Then he burst out laughing at his own joke.

"I don't need to get my hair cut for them or anyone," Grizzly pouted.

"Then don't get your haircut. But you need powder and I could use some tobacco." Longknife waited for a response that didn't come. "And you could use some sugar to make you nicer," he said, trying to get under the bearded man's skin. But Grizzly just ignored him.

"What you really need is a wife, someone to keep you warm in the winter," Longknife said, but Grizzly just shook his head. "A wife who'd tickle you into smiling more than once a century."

Longknife smelled like the burned pine cones from the Digger campfire. They'd taken a deer on the way from the rendezvous which Grizzly had shared with his Digger Indian friends. "What say we go back out for another hunt then?" Longknife asked.

"I've got enough for now," Grizzly said.

"How can you always be so sure?" Longknife asked, more in jest. His buckskins still showed the dark blood spots from the deer they'd shot.

"'Cause you should only hunt what you can carry back yourself. That's the way I set my needs," Grizzly said.

Adams' lined and haggard face made him look older than his forty-six years, reflecting the miles of trails he'd traveled since leaving Massachusetts. Longknife could only guess what the silent man had been through, knowing virtually nothing about Adams' past.

Turning to Longknife, Grizzly stroked his bushy, graying beard, pushing the hurts from the past out of his mind. "Can't believe snow's comin' this early." A flock of birds held pace with the wind, trying to outrace the coming cold.

"There's a howler comin' down from the north. I can feel it," Longknife said quietly.

Freedom circled overhead then swooped down low. Longknife watched and whispered, "Can't get over the way you got with animals."

Grizzly looked up at the eagle, then watched him fly away. A chilling wind pushed through the clearing, rattling the cabin door. Antlers on the smokehouse wall clattered with the gale winds, warning of cold days to come.

Then he saw the smoke in the distance.

CHAPTER SEVEN

Cholera

Peepers ran through the woods with the herbs he'd found. The old woman Josie was sick with cholera and he'd been doing his best to nurse her back to health.

He was an elderly man with a long grey beard and scraggly, matted, gray hair. No one knew exactly how he'd come to live in the woods, but rumor had it that he'd lost his family to smallpox and had gone crazy with grief. He'd even tattooed his chin and arms, piercing his skin and pressing charcoal into it.

Peepers seemed to appear out of nowhere, leaving herbs and nuts in front of cabins and tents, accepting bread and jerky in exchange. Since he liked to peer from bushes at people, they'd named him Peepers.

But Josie, the old woman of the mountains, was sick and he'd been doing his best to save her. Peepers had tried everything, not knowing that there was little that could be done for those that got the sickness. One either recovered or died. It was that simple.

But still Peepers wanted to try, so he'd gone into the woods to find herbs. He'd already buried Josie's husband in a clearing near the house and didn't want to bury her, so he was running as fast as his old legs would carry him to get back to the cabin to brew up herb tea.

Peepers had run into the woods when Trapper, Claw, and their renegade bunch strode into the cabin.

"There's got to be more than that old woman," Claw complained. He looked down again at Josie, who had managed to make it to the front stoop to drink from the water bucket.

"Woman's a woman," Trapper shrugged. "Bear Robe will take her."

"She's too old," Thunder said, "let's leave."

"Naw," said Trapper, taking aim, "let's at least have some fun."

"No," Thunder said, pushing up the barrel of Trapper's gun as it fired. Trapper's shot went wide.

"Now I'll have to gut her with this," Trapper said in disgust, pulling out his knife. "Or do you want to scalp her first," he grinned at Thunder.

Then they were startled by the screams of the old woman. "You should not do this!" Josie screamed, tossing her head from side to side. She'd managed to get to her feet and was walking toward them.

Trapper looked over at Claw. "She's crazy, you know."

Bridger shrugged. "Bear Robe don't care. One of those Snake Indians will take her."

Trapper started to say something cutting, but stopped. Bridger was a burly white man who was wanted for murder in the Arizona territory. His bead-work was Apache, the tribe who'd taken him in when he went on the run. He wore a fox-head cap and a dia-mond-shaped white man's scalp on his belt, which he claimed was from the man he murdered.

Trapper stood up. "Where you goin'?" Claw asked.

"Goin' to greet the little lady," Trapper said.

"You should not do this!" the woman screamed again as she got closer.

"And you ought to shut up," Trapper said, grabbing

her arm. He started to drag her towards the makeshift barn.

"No," Thunder said.

"No what?" Trapper spat out. He looked at the Indian. "You got somethin' you want to say?"

Thunder backed away. "Look," he said, pointing to the grave.

Trapper looked at the old woman's face and dropped his arm in disgust. "Cholera!" he said, trying to wipe off his hand as he backed away.

Claw's eyes went wide. "Kill her and burn the cabin," he said, not wanting anything to do with the deadly disease.

Peepers watched from the woods. He'd heard the gunshot and snuck up as close as he dared, then climbed in the crotch of a big oak tree to watch. He didn't want his friend to die but he didn't know what to do.

"Lock her in the house," Claw ordered. Thunder and his men used sticks to push her inside. Bridger brought up a flaming torch.

"Burn it now, 'fore we all get sick," Claw said. Bridger held the torch up and lit the wood thatching on the edge of the roof. The cabin caught fire.

"Hey, Claw," Bridger shouted from the rise above the cabin. "This Indian said he saw a bear print down a piece."

"So?" Claw said.

"Said it's a print with two toes missing."

Claw felt the old superstitious fear come over him. He'd thought about this moment for six long years.

About coming face-to-face with his old enemy. He thought about the paw coming down on his face, ripping it off. The pain, the agony, and the longing for revenge which had been smoldering within.

"Get the dogs," Claw said and the renegades turned to leave.

Inside the cabin, Josie slid down in a lump to the floor. She was too old to fight and too old to worry about death. With her husband dead, she had nothing to live for.

Josie didn't even feel the arms of the old man who lifted her up and carried her out from the blazing room. The smoke from the burning cabin drifted up through the hills.

CHAPTER EIGHT

Danger

Ben Franklin cocked his head, smelling the smoke on the wind. He sniffed the air, moving his head from side to side. His grizzly gray coat sparkled in the last sun of the afternoon. Eight-inch claws pulled at the air, and he stood and roared in defiance.

"What's wrong, Ben?" Grizzly asked. The big grizzly bear came over, pacing the ground next to his master.

Grizzly set his Kentucky rifle down, shifting his bullet pouch and powder horn. The leather thongs found the deep grooves in his neck from a mauling he'd taken back East by a Bengal tiger, many years before.

"He smells the smoke," Longknife said, watching the way the big bear was acting. He knew that animals had a sense of danger that he'd learned never to question.

Grizzly agreed. "Somethin' bad's happened."

Longknife watched. "You know, Griz, 'fore I met you, I'd have rather fought two Indians than one grizzly bear."

"You just got to know how to talk to 'em," Adams said. The bear nipped at the fringe on his buckskins. "What's wrong, Ben?"

The bear growled, pawing the ground. Grizzly hoped that the bear was wrong—that trouble wasn't coming. But he couldn't doubt the bear's instincts. Ben Franklin had saved his life too many times on just instinct alone.

"You goin' to sleep on me, Adams?" Longknife asked.

"No, I ain't goin' to sleep. Just thinkin', that's all."

"Well, let's think 'bout what's wrong with ol' Ben here," Longknife said, watching the pacing bear.

Ben Franklin pulled at his buckskins. "He's tryin' to tell you somethin'," Longknife said. "Either that or he's lonely," the mountain man chuckled.

"Maybe he don't like neighbors," Grizzly said.

"And maybe he's tryin' to tell you somethin' if you'd listen."

"What is it, Ben?" Grizzly asked, picking up his rifle. He felt the ancient instincts of the bear stir his blood, warning him to be careful, that danger was near.

"I told those men never to return," Grizzly frowned.

"That Trapper didn't look like the kind who listened too good. Bet the man with the ripped face you spoke 'bout is even ornerier," Longknife replied.

Grizzly looked at Ben Franklin, wondering if the bear could possibly know that Claw Wyler was somewhere out there. "Think Ben knows who we're talkin' about?"

Longknife patted the bear's head. "Ol' Ben might just take Claw's whole face off this time. Finish the job his momma started." He looked at Grizzly and grinned. "Or better yet, maybe you won't stop him and he'll finish Claw off once and for all."

Grizzly leaned down, whispering to Ben. The bear moved his head, as if listening to the conversation. Longknife started to dig at his friend again, but stopped. *He's a strange one, he is,* Longknife grinned. *Thinks he can just about talk to animals, like he's Noah hisself.*

"I'll leave in the morning," Grizzly said. He looked at Longknife. "You better go on back to your lodge now."

"But I'm comin' with you."

"No, you're not," Grizzly said.

"Yes, I am," Longknife said. "Where you go, I go. That's the deal, and besides, you need someone to help you carry back all the supplies we're gonna get from Fort Henderson."

Grizzly closed his eyes, wanting to scream. "Why don't you just go see your Buffalo Girls and leave me be for a while?"

Longknife's face brightened. "You want me to bring 'em on up? We could get hitched tonight and..."

"No," Grizzly said, walking to the edge of the ridge.

Ben Franklin followed behind, then sat up on the big rock that hung out over the edge and began pawing at the air. The grizzly bear sat back on his haunches and roared out across the hills. In an unexplainable way, he knew that the bear hunters were back.

The roar was a warning, a threat—a challenge that echoed off the rocks, cliffs and mountain tops. It was a thundering message to the bear hunters to stay away.

Ben Franklin's talons clawed the air, threatening what he'd do if they came again. It was the final warning to those who wanted to do harm to leave this valley for good. And it was a warning to the bears and animals of the valley to be ever vigilant.

And off in the distance a big gray bear answered back as it watched an old man stagger through the woods with a woman on his back. Grizzly heard the sound and saw Ben's ears perk up.

Wonder if she's back? Grizzly pondered, staring off toward the horizon.

CHAPTER NINE

Bear Track

"It's an old bear, it's got to be the one," Claw said, tracing the claw marks the Indian had found. He could hardly contain his excitement. It was a print with two toes missing and the track was fresh.

Bridger knelt down to lay his hand next to it. "Big 'nough to knock a man's head off with one swipe," the burly mountain man said. He fingered the scalp that hung from his belt.

Claw closed his eyes. *It's got to be the one*, he thought, recalling the moment when the big bear had taken half his face off. The whole scene raced through his mind and he tried to imagine what her paw would look like now.

He'd sweated a thousand nightmares, reliving the moment, seeing the bloody teeth and claws coming at him. *I know this is the same bear.* He looked at the track and then at Trapper. "What do you think?"

Trapper moved his tongue around inside his cheek. "Could be."

The dogs pulled at their leather straps. "Track looks 'bout half a day old," said Bridger.

"You're just a nitwit like the nits on that scalp," Trapper said. "Track's not more 'an two hours old."

Since dog and horsehair scalps had been sold to thrill-seeking Easterners by Indians, Bridger had left the nits infesting his trophy. It was his sure proof that his scalp was real.

"She's not too far ahead," Claw agreed, shrugging at Bridger.

The scraggly man peered out from behind the thick buffalo coat he'd taken from a settler and shook his head. "Think what you want," Bridger grumbled, running his fingers along the fine dark hair of the scalp he'd taken.

"Say," Trapper said, winking to let Claw know that he was going to have fun with Bridger, "you sure those are nits? They look like fleas to me."

Fleas were a sign that a scalp was fake, a dog scalp. Bridger took offense. "Maybe I should hang yours here."

"And maybe I should gut you on the spot," Trapper said, putting his hand on his knife.

"Stop it," Claw ordered. He looked at Trapper. "Let's see if we can get her before dark."

Bridger shifted his fox hat. "We'll have a fight on our hands with that one," he said. Claw nodded, thinking about the way the bear would foam at the mouth and fight for her life before he killed it.

Thunder looked at Claw. "We should be going," he said, still spooked by the cabin and the old woman with cholera that they had just left. The smoke from the fire drifted through the trees.

"You smell somethin'?" he asked.

Thunder cocked his head to the wind. "Animals are moving," he said. He knew that a grizzly scared small game and deer into hiding.

"Probably scared by the smoke," Trapper said.

Thunder shook his head. "They smell bear."

"So do I," Claw said, standing up.

They followed the tracks through the hills, losing

them twice in the creeks and once where other bears had crossed. But they kept going, driven by Claw's revenge.

By mid-afternoon, they saw a big, lumbering gray bear in the distance but lost the trail again. They picked it up later when they found the remains of animals the bear had eaten along the way.

It was a long, grueling day through the mountains and dense pine groves. The dogs ran ahead at full speed. It was all the men could do to keep pace.

They got close only once, at noon, when the hounds cornered the bear in the distance. But instead of climbing a tree, the bear stood its ground and fought off the dogs, mauling two dogs so badly that they were nearly dead when the men found them.

If they'd been within hearing distance, Claw would have heard the bark of the dogs, but as it was, they got there too late. All that was left were two dogs, barely alive, and Trapper's hound, who had a gash on its side and a tooth missing.

"This bear knows we're coming," said Thunder.

"It's the same bear that got me," Claw whispered, looking at the fresh tracks. "She knows I'm comin' after her."

Thunder shook his head. "We should make camp. This bear may come back."

"No, let's keep going," Bridger said. The other two Crows nodded agreement. "Let the dog go," Bridger said, looking at Trapper.

The only dog that could still run was Trapper's blue tick, black-and-tan cross hound. The dog sniffed the track, pulling to go.

"Hold back," Trapper snapped, pulling at the rope around the dog's neck. He looked at Bridger. "I ain't lettin' him go just yet. I'd rather lose one of you 'skins than my blue tick here. He's worth a lot more," he grinned, spitting on the ground at Thunder's feet.

"I want no trouble between you," Claw said. He examined the track. Each claw, each toe had made their indention.

"Let the dog go," Bridger said.

"One dog is not enough," Trapper said.

"The other two dogs are gonna die," Bridger said.

"Let the dog go," Claw said, moving out. He took the dog's lead from Trapper and set it free. The hound ran ahead, barking wildly.

"He'll find her," Claw said, heading out.

"Or maybe she'll find us," Trapper mumbled, following behind.

Thunder knelt and slit the throats of the wounded dogs. Up ahead on the trail waited a very big bear. It sniffed the ground and lumbered forward, its heavy paws making no noise on the moss-covered ground.

Claw Wyler and his men moved slowly down the cold, bleak trail. Trapper scared everyone by firing off a round.

"Why'd you shoot?" Claw asked.

Trapper shrugged. "Don't want my dog out there alone now. It's gettin' toward dark and that bear's probably hungry again."

"You treat the dog's paws?" Bridger asked. He knew that the dogs who hunted in the mountains needed their feet soaked in wild herbs to take away the soreness.

"Dog's a dog," Trapper said.

A strong wind blew down from the north. Thunder looked out over the miles of mountains ahead, wondering if the spirits were telling him to go back.

Thunder turned back toward the bear signs. "Never heard of a female bear this big," Thunder said, looking at another set of tracks.

Trapper spit again, just missing the Indian's moccasins. "And maybe you don't know the difference 'tween chicken droppings and rabbit turds."

Thunder's hair bristled at the insult. He could sense that the other two Crows were waiting to see how he would respond. *They will tell my people that I'm a coward*, he thought.

Reaching for his knife, he felt a hand on his. "Don't," said Claw, shaking his head. "He ain't worth it."

"That's right," Trapper laughed in a mocking tone, "I ain't worth losin' your scalp over." He took off his bear-head hat and rubbed the jagged scar. "Maybe you're the one who done this. Been lookin' for the Injun to get even with."

"Let up," Claw ordered.

"Okay, okay," Trapper said. "I ain't lookin' for trouble." Claw turned away, missing the sign that Trapper made to Thunder, which questioned the Indian's manliness.

"Soon," Thunder whispered, "soon we will settle this."

The air was crisp in anticipation of the coming snow.

The blue tick hound bayed in the distance. "I think my dog's found her," Trapper said.

"Move out," Claw said, taking the lead.

They tried to follow the baying dog, but were forced to zigzag a trail over rocks and streams. In the steep rough canyons, where the air was crisp, they dodged boulders tumbling toward them.

"Bear's somewhere up there, crossing a rock slide," Trapper grunted.

Claw pushed the men forward, stumbling along the river for a time as they tried to find a place to cross. But there was not a fallen log or rock line big enough and they were forced to wade across.

The rocks were too smooth to take for granted, worn smooth by the water. Bridger stumbled, going down on his knees, but Thunder kept him from wetting his powder.

"Thanks," Bridger nodded. He had no problem with the Crows, knowing that in a pinch, he'd rather have them on his side than Trapper.

The snow was coming soon and Claw was determined to make Bear Robe live up to his secret agreement. One hundred dead bears by the end of the Indian summer and the Crows would find Grizzly Adams and kill him and his bear, which Claw had convinced them would ward off the disease.

Claw knew that he was twenty bears short and had to take his battle to Grizzly Adams before the snows came. The revenge he sought burned in his soul, hurting worse than the bear's talons had felt when they'd pulled his cheek apart.

Thunder called out to Claw. "We found more tracks."

"Grizzly?"

Bridger looked down and nodded. "Grizzly tracks. A mother and a half-grown cub. Different bears than we've been trailing."

"Not as big but a good size," Thunder added.

"I'm coming," Claw shouted out. Then he looked toward the mountains, knowing that his enemy was up there somewhere. "And I'm coming for you, Grizzly Adams," he whispered into the wind.

CHAPTER TEN

Ghost Bear

Peepers made his way through the shadowy trails, carrying the old woman. He wasn't worried about cougars or Indians because he knew his friend was watching over him.

The big gray bear with the missing toes lumbered over the ridges, keeping sight of the willowy old man until he had passed through the dangerous areas on his way to Fort Henderson. Then the bear doubled back to go after the hunters.

Claw and his men followed the new tracks down the steep paths until they spotted a female grizzly bear and her cub. The bear raised her head, sniffing the wind, then went back to her foraging, trying to fatten up for the upcoming hibernation.

A loud bear's roar echoed through the hills. The female grizzly lifted her head, hearing the warning of the gray bear. Hair bristling, the mother bear realized that danger was nearby.

Claw and his men were too far away to see the scars on her head from the ferocious fights she had survived. Pulling the cub beside her, the mother grizzly cocked her head, listening and sniffing. Earlier she had smelled a strange smell, a man's smell, but the wind had taken it away.

Less than a mile away, the big gray bear with the missing toes charged through the woods. It was determined to attack the hunters.

A twig cracked in the thick brush behind the mother and cub. The mother spun around, growling, trying to find where the sound came from.

Claw Wyler braced his rifle on a fallen tree.

"It ain't the big bear but it's a grizzly," Trapper whispered.

"That's all that counts with Bear Robe," Claw said, holding his aim steady. The air felt like a snow dusting was coming, and an early blizzard might trap them in the hills.

Trapper heard the roar of the big bear and knew it was getting closer. He shivered, tightening his coat. "That big bear's out there somewhere," he whispered. "I say we shoot this one and skeedaddle."

"First this one, then the other," Claw said.

"That all?" Trapper said sarcastically.

"Nope," Claw said, taking aim, "then we get Grizzly Adams and his bear."

From the ridge above, the big bear roared again. The Crows looked around in fear. Claw motioned for them to get down. "That momma bear's sniffing for us," he said, watching the bear spin around, trying to protect her cub.

"Don't matter, she's just about dead," Trapper mumbled.

His hound dog growled at his side, wanting to attack. "Not yet, not yet," Trapper grinned, stroking the dog's ears.

"She's got your dog's scent," Claw mumbled, watching the bear turn in circles.

Trapper cocked his rifle. "*Had* the scent," he grinned, preparing to fire with both eyes open, as was his style.

"Watch out!" Bridger screamed as the big bear came crashing through the bushes at them, knocking Claw backwards and crushing Bridger's chest with one mighty swipe.

Trapper tried to fire, but the bear knocked the rifle from his hands. The mother bear and her cub raced off into the woods as the big bear came at Trapper, swatting the air with her paws.

"Shoot!" Trapper yelled to Thunder. But the Crow hesitated, enjoying Trapper's fear. The grizzly lunged, thrusting her huge head, snapping her jaws. The dog jumped at the bear but wasn't fast enough. The bear ripped it in half.

"She killed my dog!" Trapper shouted. Bridger moaned, reaching out for help, but Trapper stepped over him.

The grizzly had the dog in its jaws and shook it about like a rag doll. Crazed with anger, Trapper rushed headlong toward the bear, plunging his Bowie knife deep into its shoulder.

The bear dropped the dog and thrust its talons at Trapper, swiping down his back. Trapper ducked, but the sharp talons ripped his buckskin shirt open, leaving rivers of blood running down his back.

Claw stood on the side, trying to cock his rifle, but the hammer was bent. "Gimme a gun!" he shouted to the Indians. But they were too scared to move.

The bear arched her back, trying to dislodge Trapper's knife. She rolled on the ground but the knife only dug deeper. When she stood up again, she charged at the Indians, knocking one over and opening the chest of the other with a swipe of her claws. The Indian died, trying to hold his insides back.

"You killed my dog!" Trapper screamed at the bear. He took the dead Indian's knife and raised it. The bear charged forward, swiping at Trapper's face, drawing blood.

"Kill it," Claw ordered.

"You kill it," Trapper said, staggering back. He looked wildly around for a weapon. Trapper felt the blood run down his cheek. He looked at Thunder and said darkly, "Shoot, damn you."

Thunder looked at Trapper, giving the bear the opening to charge forward, mouth foaming, snarling in anger. She knocked Thunder down, then tossed the other Crow away like a doll.

The bear charged after Trapper. "Shoot her!" he screamed.

Claw fired but didn't hit a vital spot. Ten feet tall, the bear kept pressing forward, trying to get to Trapper. Trapper ran for his life, desperate to escape.

The huge beast chased Trapper through the brush, knocking away small trees and branches. Trapper knew there was no advantage in running from a bear, because they always won.

"Shoot her, damn you!" he shouted back to Claw.

Claw raised his rifle and took aim. Thunder watched, hoping that Claw would not waste the bullet. But Claw didn't want to be without his crazy man in Indian country and he took a bead on the bear's neck.

He knew that if he didn't kill the bear with this shot, that the huge grizzly would rip Trapper to pieces. Claw pulled the trigger but the hammer just clicked.

"Misfired, damn," he mumbled, grabbing Thunder's gun.

Trapper screamed obscenities, swearing what he'd do if someone didn't help him. Claw cocked back the rifle, aimed quickly, fired again, but hit the bear's side.

The bear spun around, giving Trapper the chance to escape. He climbed a pine tree, scurrying straight to the top, figuring that the bear was too wounded to climb. Claw fired again but the bear just swatted at her side.

"Die, damn you," Claw muttered.

The big bear stopped, rose up on her legs one last time and roared out her hurt and anger. Claw and Thunder watched as she pawed the air. Then she was gone.

"That bear should have been dead," Claw mumbled.

"Maybe she's already dead," Thunder said. "Maybe she's a ghost bear and she's come back to haunt you."

Thunder rubbed his medicine bag. Something bad was going to happen—he could feel it. *There would be no coups to sing about from this hunt.*

CHAPTER ELEVEN

Burial Time

Peepers carried Josie along the last part of the trail. "Hold on," he whispered," We're almost at the fort." But she was already dead.

"I'll bury you proper," he said, choking back tears. She'd been good to him and he wouldn't leave her on the trail for the wolves.

He made his way across a creek and up a rise. "There's a churchyard here you'd like," he said.

Fort Henderson lay nestled between the hills, a small trading community located on a natural river and trail crossing. Like all western towns, it was a link to keep the frontier going.

It had grown from little more than a trading post to a thriving small town. Farmers came from more than fifty miles away to sell produce and buy goods. The trappers and mountain men came in after the spring and fall hunts with wagonloads of hides and animal fat to be made into tallow.

Built on the crossroads of the hunting trails that led to the Pacific Northwest and those that headed east toward the Colorado mountains, Fort Henderson was a natural stopping point for anyone coming through the territory.

Now, with cholera sweeping through the hills, the town was vigilant in keeping away the sick ones. They'd turned away wagon trains with sick people and drank only rainwater, worried about the epidemic of cholera that had spread along the Platte River.

Gold seekers and settlers had carried the disease

across the continent, leaving a westward path marked by graves. It was called the lonely disease, because the pioneers and hill people died by themselves, without physicians, ministers, or friends.

The men of the town had erected a gate to stop people from entering. Doc Watters, the town doctor, inspected new arrivals to determine who was sick, but he was fighting a losing battle, since the disease had already added thirty-nine new graves to the town cemetery.

The closer Peepers got, the more subdued the town appeared. The streets were deserted and some of the stores were boarded up. Crudely written signs tacked to trees and hitching posts that led toward the fort's entrance issued this warning:

CHOLERA SICKLY KEEP OUT— BY ORDER OF SHERIFF EVERYONE WILL BE INSPECTED

Peepers couldn't read but he knew that something bad had happened. There just didn't seem to be much life to the town where he occasionally sold his herbs and wild berries.

He carried his old friend to the edge of the town and stopped when a man with a rifle challenged him. "Who you be?"

Peepers nodded toward the woman in his arms. "Speak up," said the man, trying to get a better view. Then his eyes went wide.

"She's dead," the man whispered. "She's got the cholera."

Peepers nodded. He'd tried to bring her to town in the hope that a doctor could help her, but she'd died a half-mile back. Now he just wanted to bury her in the church cemetery.

"Please," Peepers whispered, "I...I...I want to take her to the church."

"Get outta here with her," the guard said, pointing his gun. "Go burn her body. Get her outta here!"

Doc Watters came out. "Go on back, Doc," the guard said. "This one's leavin'. She's already dead."

The doctor shivered. The disease had already passed through the town, and he figured that if they just kept out any more sick ones, then the rest of the residents of Fort Henderson had a good chance of surviving if he could get more medicine.

Doc Watters took a long breath. "Wish he were bringin' a load of laudanum. We're 'bout out." He knew that the tincture of opium and camphor was the only thing that seemed to work, but they were running low.

"When's that wagon train gettin' here?" the guard asked. "It's got some on it, don't it?"

Doc Watters nodded. "The wagon train's got the laudanum but if it don't get here soon, I won't be able to help the sick kids. Then the disease will spread and..." he shook his head not wanting to think about burying more people.

Peepers held up the dead woman, but Doc Watters waved him away. "Take her into the woods. Bury her fast and pray that you don't get the cholera."

Peepers nodded slowly, then turned back toward the

trail. The road to the town had been like a graveyard, with makeshift graves and crosses dotting the hills. He would find a place to bury his friend, then go back to find the men who burned her house down.

Back across the hills, Claw looked at Trapper. "Sorry 'bout your dog," he said.

Trapper shrugged. "Dog's a dog. One less mouth to feed, that's all he is to me now."

"You want me to have them bury it?"

Trapper laughed. "I'll just use his old carcass as trap bait," he said, carrying the dog off by its leg. Claw watched him take a trap from his pack.

He's serious, Claw thought. Trapper's coldness and lack of feeling bothered Claw. He was driven to kill Grizzly Adams for revenge, not, like Trapper, by a sick blood lust to kill anything that breathed.

Trapper didn't care whether Grizzly Adams lived or died. He hadn't come along to hunt Grizzly Adams, just grizzly bears. Claw's revenge was not his affair.

Bridger reached out his hands. "Help me, Claw, I'm gonna die."

Claw spat in disgust. "Help yourself, I got things to do," he said, looking off in the direction the big bear went. Thunder knelt down and whispered something to Bridger. Bridger moaned and his head slumped to the ground. Thunder reached to touch him, but it was too late.

When Trapper came back, he asked, "We already got eighty skins back at the camp, ain't that 'nough for Bear Robe?"

One of the Indians came over, showing a bloody bear tooth that the big gray bear had lost. Claw took the tooth and slipped it into the possible-sack that hung from his belt.

He looked at Trapper. "That big bear would have finished us off. Now we need 'bout twenty more grizzlies before we can go after Grizzly Adams and his bear." His fingers traced the scars on his face.

Trapper shook his head. The encounter with the big bear had scared him. "I think goin' after Grizzly Adams is risky. These are his woods."

"So?"

"So, I say we take the loot we got waitin' from the Crows and head to Frisco for the winter. Been a long time since I been with a woman."

"No woman would want you the way you stink," Claw said. Trapper, like most mountain men, rarely bathed. But Trapper smelled worse than anyone else because he liked to cover himself with the essence of the animals he killed.

"I may stink, but I don't get bug bites." Then Trapper frowned. "What say we go back to Bear Robe and take our loot and skeedaddle? Snow's comin'. I can feel it."

Claw shook his head. "I want to kill Adams' bear and then I'll take care of Mr. Grizzly Adams hisself."

"If you're man enough," Trapper teased. Then he got serious. "You want we should bury Bridger?"

"Do it if you want," Claw said.

"Don't matter nothin' to me. Didn't much like the man anyhow."

He looked at the dead man and said quietly, "What good's buryin' someone anyway? You just drop 'em in a hole so the maggots can eat 'em." He turned and looked at the dead Crow. "What 'bout the dead Indian?"

Claw shrugged. "Thunder will take care of his own."

Thunder and his comrade carried the dead Crow into the woods. After they came back, Claw led them back toward their camp.

A gray wolf stood on the far ledge above them, howling.

"Eat well, my brother," Thunder whispered, knowing it smelled the dead white man they'd left behind. Soon the air was filled with unearthly howls.

Though it sounded like a hundred wolves, Thunder knew that it was just three or four in the hills, sniffing the dead. Trapper saw the wolf in the distance and wanted to shoot it, but Claw stopped him. "Don't waste the shot."

"Hate wolves," Trapper muttered, remembering a cold night on the run from a Nevada sheriff when a hungry pack of wolves had killed his horse and tried to eat him.

Then the wolves went silent. It happened so suddenly that all the men spooked. "What's wrong?" Claw asked, looking around.

Trapper nodded with his head. Standing on a ledge in the distance was the big bear that had attacked them. The bear with the half-missing paw.

"Damn thing looks like a ghost," Claw whispered. The big bear roared out over the hills, challenging Claw to come at her again.

Thunder began chanting quietly. "Shut up!" Trapper snapped, pointing his rifle at the bear. The tic on his cheek twitched wildly.

"Can you hit her?" Claw asked Trapper.

"Maybe, maybe not," Trapper shrugged.

Claw looked at Trapper's rifle. "Yours don't got 'nough power," he said, looking at Trapper's Hankins rifle. He knew that with the target three hundred yards away the gun was underpowered.

"You just watch," Trapper mumbled.

While the Sharps breech-loader was the weapon of choice in the West, Trapper liked his old percussion system. Claw handed over his Sharps rifle, but Trapper shook his head. He'd had his rifle bored to a larger caliber, strengthened the wrist and shortened the stock to what was commonly called a Plains rifle.

Claw held his breath, whispering, "Don't miss." The Crows nodded in agreement. No one wanted a big wounded grizzly bear in the hills, especially a monster beast like this one.

The huge bear roared again, then turned to leave. Trapper aimed with both eyes open, then slowly pulled the trigger as the bear turned to face them one last time. Her movement was enough to move her vital target points so that Trapper only grazed her. She spun around, raging in pain, pawing the air.

"Missed," Thunder smiled, amused that Trapper had failed.

"Gimme that Sharps," Trapper said, reaching for Claw's rifle, but before he could get off a second shot, the monster bear was gone.

"Let's follow and kill it," Claw said.

"No," Trapper said sternly. "It'll be dark soon. We'll just have to come back with more dogs."

"No good to hunt a wounded bear in the dark," Thunder said, picking up his load.

They made their way back to where they'd left the other two Crows with their hobbled horses and pack mules. The skins of eighty bears were tied and ready to load by first light.

With the snow coming, Claw knew he wasn't going to get twenty more bears, which meant that Bear Robe wouldn't send his braves to kill Adams or the big bear. So he'd have to do it on his own.

Revenge will be mine, said the Lord, Claw grinned. *But the real revenge is what I've been savin' for Adams. Gonna kill him slow, then I'm gonna kill that bear and whoever else is standin' with him.*

They heard the wounded bear roar, each man knowing that they had left the most dangerous animal on earth in a wounded rage.

"Glad we're going," Trapper mumbled. "Don't like feeling like the one bein' hunted."

The big bear with the mangled paw charged through the woods, snapping branches, splintering small trees. She rubbed against the big pines to stop the pain which burned in her side from the bullets, then rolled in the mud until the wounds were covered.

With the stealth of a far smaller animal, the big bear began following along the ridge watching the men below. She was stalking her prey and could taste the kill already.

CHAPTER TWELVE

Buffalo Girls

Grizzly Adams did everything he could to get Longknife to go back to his lodge for the night, but the man seemed determined to stay and sleep on his floor again. "Look Longknife, why don't you just go take a walk. I need some time to think."

"Okay, okay," Longknife said, "I know when I'm not wanted 'round here."

"No you don't," Grizzly muttered under his breath.

Longknife turned. "You say somethin', Griz?" Adams shook his head. "You want maybe to take care of Yankee and Doodle?" he asked, lifting the ferrets from his carry-sack. Grizzly shook his head no. "Okay, I'll just take a little stroll and then come on back. See if you're in a more hospitable mood."

Longknife took off in the direction of the Diggers camp, so Grizzly figured he wouldn't see him until the next day. *Maybe I can sneak out at first light and not have to bring him along.* Grizzly didn't want to be slowed down. He wanted to see if Claw Wyler and his men had dared to return to his mountains.

Grizzly sat in his cabin, rocking slowly back and forth in the mountain rocker he'd made. Bandit sat on his lap and Ben lay by his side. The cabin had expanded into two rooms and a small food storage room that had a heavy wooden door. Antlers hung over the cook fire and primitive tools lined the walls. There was an old leather Bible on a wooden slab table in the corner, along with a copy of *Pilgrim's Progress*, which Grizzly had read three times. *The Farmer's Almanac* sat beside it.

On the makeshift mantle above the cook fire, Longknife had left a copy of the dime novel that had been written about Grizzly's exploits. Neither mountain man had any idea that the story of Grizzly Adams was the talk of the East.

Grizzly walked over and picked it up, looking at the title:

LIFE OF J.C. ADAMS

Known as Grizzly Adams, Containing a Truthful Account of his Bears, Fights with Poachers, Hairbreadth Escapes in the Rocky and Nevada Mountains and the Wilds of the Pacific Northwest.

Grizzly opened to the chapter titled, "Saving His Scalp," and began reading:

Riding through a steep mountain ravine in the Northern Sierras, Grizzly Adams rode on, trying to keep ahead of the savage Indians. His coonskin hat had been shot off by a flaming arrow, he had a bullet in his back and was bleeding from a knife wound in his arm. Ben, his faithful grizzly bear, raced ahead, roaring at the Indians who were hiding in the bushes. Grizzly Adams still had five miles of bad road to go before he got to the fort. And though any other mortal man would have been dead, Grizzly Adams was alive, because he was the toughest mountain man of them all.

"Can't believe people would want to read such things," he said, putting it down. "I don't even like riding horses."

He thought about Longknife.

"Imagine that man sayin' I needed a wife," he snorted, "and a pack of kids! What could I teach a boy?" he wondered, sitting back down in the rocker. Bandit pulled at his shirt fringe, wanting to play.

"Only thing a man can teach a boy is what's in his heart and head, things he's learned in life. What a boy does with it is his own doin'." Grizzly let out a long stream of air, thinking about all his failed ventures. "I've got nothin' to tell 'bout 'cept heartache and failin' in the world."

Ben pawed at his feet, and Grizzly nodded. "I didn't learn nothin' until I came to the woods. Then I learned that there are the laws of civilization and the laws of the woods—laws that you set for yourself, to test yourself, to keep your life straight."

He realized that he was lonely in ways that no one else could imagine. That what he really needed was to share his experiences with someone so they wouldn't make the same mistakes.

Suddenly Grizzly heard a commotion outside. Longknife had showed up with the two Digger Indian sisters, the ones he called the Buffalo Girls, breaking Grizzly's silence.

"Hey, Griz, come on out here," Longknife called out.

Grizzly closed his eyes, not wanting any company. "Go back to your lodge. I want to be left alone." Then he heard giggles.

Longknife knocked on the door. "Got you someone who wants to talk to you. Got her papa chief here also."

Grizzly walked slowly to the door. Standing there were Longknife, two heavyset Digger Indian girls and their father. "Evenin'" he said, nodding out of respect to the elder Indian. The Indian greeted him back.

Longknife spoke up. "This is part of the courtship they do. Bringin' the daughter to the lodge of the future husband, to see if he's okay."

Grizzly shook his head. "Not tonight."

"You got to, Griz," Longknife whispered, "or they'll be insulted."

Grizzly looked at the girls. One could hardly face him without blushing. Grizzly moved aside as one of the Buffalo Girl's pushed him out of the way to peek at what was inside.

Longknife chuckled.

"Would you be quiet," Grizzly said, embarrassed that one of the girls kept looking at him.

"That one's yours," he grinned. "She's 'bout as big as Ben but a whole lot nicer." Ben growled at the mention of his name.

Before Grizzly could speak, the two sisters pushed through the door and began poking around Grizzly's cabin. Longknife patted Grizzly on the back as the girls giggled, picking up what few clothes Grizzly had.

"Might be a little crowded in here for the four of us, but we'll manage," Longknife said.

Grizzly's eyes went wide. "Don't even think 'bout that."

Longknife just kept right on talking. "'Course, we could add ourselves another couple rooms, one for me and my little princess to sleep in and maybe a loft for you and your little honeybee and...and one for all the kids and..."

Grizzly turned with and looked at Longknife with fire in his eyes. "I didn't ask you to get involved with my life. You understand?"

Longknife slowly shook his head. "And I didn't ask you to save mine, but you did, and now I owe you, do you understand?"

The two men stared at each other until the Indian chief joined them. Forced to be polite, Grizzly gave them food and drink, but he was relieved when they left shortly after that.

After they'd said good-bye, Longknife stood with Grizzly on the rock step, watching them head back to their village. "How'd you learn that tongue-twistin' language anyway?"

"I listen instead of talkin', which is somethin' you'd know nothin' 'bout."

Longknife heard wolves in the distance and shivered. "Guess it's too late for me to be headin' back to my lodge. Guess I'll just sleep here again if you don't mind."

"I mind."

"You wouldn't send a man out when there's a pack of man-eatin' wolves out there, runnin' 'round, lookin' to eat someone, would ya?"

Grizzly heard the wolves. It sounded like a pack of them running across the ridge. "This is the last night," he said disgustedly.

After they'd gotten ready for the night, Longknife sat up from his bedroll, listening to the wolves. Ben Franklin heard the howling and pushed open the door. He went to the edge of the ridge and roared out a warning. It was echoed by the cougars and other animals of the night.

Longknife groaned. "How can you sleep with all that racket going on? Sounds like Africa."

"Thought you said you never been there," Grizzly said, not looking at him.

"That's right, but my father told me 'bout my grandfather, who hunted monster beasts over there. Beasts so big that they make your bear look like a church mouse."

Grizzly Adams frowned. "Go to sleep."

But Longknife was off on another brag. "Yes sir, in Africa, they have lions that are one hundred feet long and fifty feet high. They eat thirty sheep just for breakfast." Grizzly snored, pretending to sleep. "And they have dragons so big that they can eat up a train."

Grizzly looked over and said, "Dragons? There's no such thing."

"How do you know that? Have you ever been to Africa?"

"No, and you ain't been there either."

"But I got the blood and I heard 'bout African dragons, which makes me more of an expert than you, don't it?"

"Whatever you say," Grizzly said, rolling over and covering his head with his blanket.

Longknife laid down, but Ben roared again at the

howling wolves. "Ain't that noise wakin' you up?"

"You're the only one wakin' me up."

"You wanna talk some more 'bout what we're gonna do in Fort Henderson? I might even spring and get you a bath and a haircut."

"I'll do my own bathin', thank you."

"We'll get a couple hot tubs pulled and sit back and have ourselves a drink. Smell good for a change."

"Go to sleep."

Longknife lay down, then sat up again. "How come you still wear those miner's drawers?"

Grizzly looked up. "How you know what underwear I got on?"

Longknife grinned. "You had 'em on the first night I stayed over, and the next and I saw 'em again tonight 'fore you turned in. Don't you ever change them things or are they stuck to you?" he chuckled.

"I wash, which is more than I can say for you."

Longknife shrugged. "You won't catch me stickin' my black behind in those ice-cold streams you sit in."

"Wakes you up," Grizzly grinned.

Longknife shook his head. "No sir, I value my privates more that freezin' 'em in those ice-cold streams you do your bathin' in. Me, why, I'll wait till we get to Fort Henderson and take a nice long soak."

"Hope you do it soon, 'cause you kinda stink," Grizzly mumbled.

Longknife rolled around, trying to get comfortable. "Why you don't have beds in here, I'll never know. Good host always has a bed to offer to friends."

"I don't have beds cause I don't need friends."

Longknife chuckled in the dark. "Good night, friend."

"Will you quit callin' me your friend."

"I think you're upset 'cause you're in love with your little honeybee. She's sweet on you, I can tell."

"I ain't in love," Grizzly snapped.

"Okay, okay, Griz, whatever you say."

"My name's not Griz."

"What should I call you then? Bear man?"

"Name's Adams, Grizzly Adams."

"How'd you get that name anyway?" Grizzly didn't answer. "What if you liked rabbits? Would they call you Bunny Adams? Or what if you kept pigs around, would they call you Hog Adams?" Longknife broke up laughing at his own jokes, but Grizzly Adams didn't say anything. He didn't like being the brunt of Longknife's humor.

"Folks down in Fort Henderson know you're a shoemaker?" Longknife teased.

"Should never have told you 'bout that," Grizzly muttered, wanting to think about something besides Longknife and Claw Wyler. "And I should never have gone to that rendezvous," he mumbled.

"Then you'd have never met me." Longknife waited for an answer. "You say somethin', Griz?"

"No."

"Okay," Longknife whispered. "Goodnight neighbor. We're gonna have fun at Fort Henderson, aren't we?"

"Goin' by myself."

"Okay," Longknife sighed, rolling over in disgust. "You go off to sleep in a bad mood."

CHAPTER THIRTEEN

First Light

While Longknife cut strips of jerky and hard bread, Grizzly built up enough wood for coals in the fireplace and smokehouse to last until he returned. Like a good mountain man, he never let his fire go out.

Bandit and the ferrets rolled in the corners playing. "Bandit, who's gonna feed you while we're gone?" Longknife wondered aloud. The raccoon scampered over to the food room, unhinged the door and went in. A moment later he came out with a piece of bread in his hands, gobbling away.

Grizzly came in, pulling from an odd-shaped loaf. "You want some of my bread?" Grizzly asked, holding out what remained of a load of grass-seed bread that the Digger Indians had left on the step.

Longknife made a face. "More like birdseed bread," he said, disgustedly, flapping his wings like a chicken. "'Bout as bad as that acorn coffee you gave me this morning."

"You should have sweetened it with pine sugar," Grizzly said.

"I'll use that as tar on a canoe, but my stomach don't need to be sweetened with that death juice," Longknife grumbled. "Least your rabbit sausage was passable for an Easterner." He looked at his friend. "Why can't you learn to make good sourdough biscuits like normal people eat? Even Apache bread is better than that grass-seed dirt bread you make."

"You better get to like Digger bread if you're talkin' 'bout marryin' one."

Longknife shook his head. "I'm gonna teach them to make cornbread, good stuff like that."

"Where you gonna get corn up here?" Grizzly asked.

Longknife shrugged. "I'll figure a way.

After closing the cabin and painting the Digger Indian sign to keep out, they headed down the trail. Freedom circled overhead, then followed at a distance.

"You know, Griz," Longknife said as they crossed over a shallow stream, "maybe I should teach you how to cook buffalo hump or roast beaver tail."

"Hump's okay, but I don't like beaver tail. It stinks when you cook it."

"Smells bad but tastes good," Longknife grinned. "I just hold my nose when I eat it. Gotta teach Little Princess to cook."

Ben Franklin raced ahead, pushing through the underbrush. The air smelled of pine needles which made a soft carpet as they walked the trails. The clear Sierra air had a nip of cold in it, which opened Adams' lungs like a tonic.

Longknife saw the smoke from the Digger's cook fires. "Those Diggers are sure nice. They 'bout gave me the whole village when I was down there."

"That's their way," Grizzly nodded.

He knew that ignorance of the Indian ways was the cause of most problems between the settlers and tribes. The whites coming West didn't know that it was the custom of most Indians to offer tokens of hospitality, gifts and food to those that came through their lands. But they expected gifts in return, which the settlers in their wagons thought was begging. This in turn led to hostility and eventually to fighting.

Grizzly had made it a point to understand the Indians whose land he traveled through, figuring it had saved his life more than a few times. At the edge of the Diggers village, several of the hunters came out and told them about seeing a small band of Crows and white men hunting in the woods together. Longknife listened, trying to figure out what they were saying.

"You mind tellin' me what all that jawbonin' was 'bout?" he asked when the Diggers walked away.

Grizzly thought for a moment, then said, "They saw three white men and three Indians hunting the ghost bear but only four men come out."

"Maybe the others are still 'round here," Longknife said, looking around.

"Don't think so," Grizzly said. "Diggers said they fought the bear and that later the wolves howled in a feeding frenzy."

"Maybe they shot the big bear."

"No, they said the ghost bear walked by their camp last night under the moon."

Longknife waved it all off. "Ghost bear? You're talkin' like one of the Diggers."

"I am," Grizzly said, "in my own way."

The Buffalo Girls came out, giggling around Longknife. Then a group of young braves came out, asking him to play Bone Up. Grizzly stood back, watching as Longknife took a small bag of bones from his pouch and rolled them on the ground.

He looked at the bones with a flourish of his hands, making exaggerated expressions, then told the Indians that they were going to be great hunters, warriors, and lovers.

They all patted Longknife on the back and stuck plugs of tobacco into his pouch. Grizzly watched them walk away happy, then asked. "What was that all about?"

"I was playin' Bone Up."

"Bone Up? What the heck's that?"

Longknife smiled. "It's an old African game I learned from my uncle. You roll the bones and interpret the future."

"Does it work?" Grizzly asked skeptically.

Longknife couldn't help but laugh. "I just tell them what they want to hear. A happy man always pays faster than a sad man."

After Longknife finished flirting with the Buffalo Girls, they headed down the trail toward where the Diggers had said the men had fought the big bear. Longknife started to sing, but Grizzly stopped him.

"No more singin'. I'm gettin' to hate that song," he said.

"But I like "Yankee Doodle." Makes me and my ferrets feel good." The two ferrets stuck their heads out of the carry-sack.

"Just be quiet. Those men might still be around."

They walked in silence for the next half hour, passing several cholera graves which they gave a wide berth. They stopped at a cabin where Grizzly knew the people, but found only graves outside and the house taken over by animals and bees.

Half an hour later, after they'd crossed over a log that

had fallen across a river, Ben began to growl. Longknife nodded toward Freedom, who was circling just over the ridge.

"I smell smoke," Longknife whispered and Grizzly nodded.

They crept silently, using the soft bed of pine needles to cover their footsteps, then came to a burned-out cabin. Peepers was sitting cross-legged in front of it.

Grizzly looked around, but felt it was safe and he moved forward. "Peepers, what happened?" he asked the old man.

"Dead," he mumbled. Then Peepers looked up. "Josie is dead too."

Grizzly knew that the old woman of the cabin had befriended Peepers. "I'm sorry. Was it the cholera?" Peepers nodded. "

You burn down the cabin?"

Grizzly waited for an answer, then Peepers shook his head slowly back and forth.

"Man with half a face did it," he whispered.

Longknife stood behind Grizzly. "He's talkin' 'bout Claw and the renegades."

"You're right." Ben Franklin sniffed the air, then ran down toward the stream. "You gonna be all right, Peepers?" Grizzly asked.

"Just sayin' good-bye," he whispered, then turned back toward the cabin.

"Be careful," Grizzly said, "these are bad men that did this."

They tried to keep up with Ben but the bear had raced far ahead. Freedom was nowhere in sight. When they crossed through a steep break in the rocks, they found Ben sniffing the ground, circling around, very excited.

"Wounded bear," Longknife said, looking at the bloody track.

"Not just any bear," Grizzly said, pointing to the print with two missing toes.

"That's your dang ghost bear, isn't it?"

Grizzly nodded. "Ben's mother."

Longknife measured the depth of the track with his index finger. "Must weigh two tons," he said, shaking his head at the thought of a bear that big. "Probably 'bout as big as a baby African dragon, maybe even half the size of the most dangerous animal on earth."

Grizzly looked up. "This is the most dangerous animal on earth," he said, pointing to the track.

"Grizzlies are mean, but in Africa, you got the crocallo. Now that's dangerous."

"The what?"

"The crocallo. Half crocodile and half water buffalo. 'Bout fifty feet long, twenty feet high, and eats all the white men it can find."

"Then you'd have no problem," Grizzly teased.

"That's why Africa is black, 'cause the crocallo ate up all the whites." Then Longknife chuckled. "Could use us a few of the crocallos down in the slave states. Help even the odds. What you think?"

"I think we need to get movin'," Grizzly said.

Longknife measured the bear track against his palm. "From what I've heard round the camps, this bear is a man killer."

"And she'll kill more if she's badly wounded," Grizzly said.

Ben Franklin ran ahead and began growling. Longknife followed and knelt down where the bear was sniffing. "Looks like six men passed this way," he said, pointing east and four men passed this way," he said, pointing west.

Grizzly studied the tracks. "Looks like the same men goin' both directions." Longknife nodded, thinking about what the Diggers had said about six men going in and only four men coming back.

"What tribe?" Longknife asked.

Grizzly studied the curved shape. He'd learned how to tell the tribe by the shape of the moccasin track, and whether a man was running or walking by the impression the ball of the foot made. "These here are Crows," he said.

Longknife nodded. "The ones runnin' with Claw Wyler. All them are renegades." He kept his eyes on the woods. "They could still be around."

Grizzly looked back toward the path the wounded bear had taken. "Either we follow the wounded bear or follow the men. Can't do both."

For Longknife, there was no choice. "I ain't gonna follow no wounded grizzly ghost monster bear. No decision to be made there if you're askin' me."

Grizzly looked at Longknife. "I ain't askin' you."

"Then why'd you ask?" Longknife said.

"I didn't."

"You sure did," Longknife sighed. "You said, either we follow that bear or follow the men. Can't do both.

That's what you said, 'cause I heard it."

Grizzly knew he shouldn't leave a wounded bear around, but he didn't have time to argue with his talkative, uninvited traveling companion.

"We'll come back for the bear," Grizzly said, pushing ahead to the tracks that the six men had left when they'd come into the woods.

"*You'll* follow the bear," Longknife mumbled. "Don't like this *we'll* stuff at all."

"Thought we were neighbors," Grizzly smiled.

"Visitin' neighbors, not ghost bear huntin' neighbors," Longknife said.

They lost the trail when they came to a river that they then had to wade across. "Get ready for your cold bath," Grizzly said, stripping off his pants.

"And get ready to finally takin' off them miner's underpants," Longknife grinned.

Grizzly slipped off his buckskins and underbritches. Longknife took off his pants, but had on another pair underneath.

"Do you always wear two pairs of pants?" Grizzly asked.

Longknife shrugged. "Never know when I'll be playin' the ferret game," he said, slipping out of the second pair.

Stripped from feet to waist, they held their moccasins, guns, and clothing above their heads and carefully waded across the glassy stones. Ben Franklin swam ahead toward the other side, then stood on the bank, shaking his thick coat off.

"Hope there ain't no leeches in here," Longknife

mumbled, feeling the rush of icy cold water that was numbing his waist.

"No leeches," Grizzly said, pushing ahead, "but there's a lot of worm eatin' snapping turtles."

"Move out of my way," Longknife said, pushing forward to get out of the waist-high water.

On the other side they picked up the trail of the men and made good time. They pushed through the pine stands and ridges, through the dwarf juniper and wild cherry bushes, then came to a thick stand of scrub pine. Vultures circled overhead.

Ben Franklin charged ahead, growling at the bushes. A frightened group of vultures and scavengers flew away in a rush and a wolf, covered with gore, charged out growling.

"Somethin's there," Longknife whispered, pinching his nose as the stinking wolf raced by baring its teeth.

The two mountain men crept forward and found Ben Franklin sniffing what was left of a man's rotting carcass. "They didn't even bury him," Longknife noted.

Grizzly looked at the prints, signs of the fight that had gone on. "This is where they fought the bear, where the two men died."

Longknife looked around. "Where's the other body?"

Grizzly shrugged. "Diggers said a Crow didn't come back from the fight. They probably took their own out into the woods and covered him over."

"Funny them white men leavin' their own to be ripped apart by wolves," Longknife said, then he pushed Grizzly over shouting, "Watch it!" as a big wolf leaped out.

Grizzly hit his shoulder against the rocks but the shove from Longknife had saved his life. Longknife shot the wolf in mid-air and it rolled off dead into the bushes.

"Thanks," Grizzly said, dusting himself off.

"See, that's why you need me along," Longknife grinned.

"Now your debt's repaid. You saved my life, you don't owe me no more."

"Good," Longknife said, "now we can be friends on an equal basis. Owin' you was startin' to bother me."

They covered the man's remains with rocks, said a prayer, then continued on, following the tracks of the four men who'd survived the fight with the ghost bear.

"I warned Claw to stay out of my mountains," Grizzly said.

"Guess he don't listen too good." A cold wind shot down through the hills. "Might be a long trail 'fore we catch up to 'em," Longknife said. "They might even get out of your valley before the snow comes."

"We're not more than a day behind them," Grizzly said, putting his fur hat on.

Longknife shook his head. "If we don't catch them soon, they'll be gone 'till the spring. That is," he said, kicking his moccasin in the dirt, "if they don't catch us first."

Not more than a quarter-mile down the trail, they found a panther sniffing around the dead blue tick hound in the steel trap. Grizzly scared the animal away and Longknife sprang the trap with a stick.

"What kind of man would leave a trap like this behind, when they're not huntin' for meat?" Longknife asked.

Grizzly Adams took the trap and broke it against the rocks. "A crazy man."

"Trapper," Longknife stated, as if the very name conjured up bad memories. "The man with the broken brains."

"Maybe we can catch up by nightfall," Grizzly said, starting on the trail again. "It looks like they're headin' toward Fort Henderson."

"Good, let's go there and we can get a soak and buy our sweeties some treats." Grizzly ignored him. They walked in silence for a quarter mile, then Longknife said, "That's a lot of miles to cover by nightfall."

Grizzly shrugged. "I'm a long way from Medfield, Massachusetts, so a few more miles ain't gonna hurt."

As they walked along, Longknife joked. "I still can't imagine you being from Mass-ass-chu-setts. And a cobbler no less. A shoemaker! How'd you ever get out here anyway?"

"It's a long story," Grizzly said, not wanting to talk about it.

"That's what you always say," Longknife complained. "One day I'm gonna hog-tie you and won't let you go 'til I hear it all—the whole story."

"Then read that dime novel that reporter wrote 'bout me," Grizzly smiled. He knew that Longknife had looked at the pictures a dozen times.

Like most of the mountain men, Longknife couldn't read. Though he could recite the events of an entire hunt, he had resisted learning to read.

Longknife shook his head. "I keep tellin' you. I can't read. You got to read it to me."

"When we get to Fort Henderson, I'll leave you over at the school."

"No," Longknife said stubbornly, "I'm too old to read." He muttered along for a few steps, then said, "What you want to read for anyway?"

"'Cause it takes you places in your mind. Places where you might never go but feel you been after readin' 'bout it."

"Oh yeah, like where?" Longknife said, defensively.

Grizzly heard the honking of geese heading south for the winter. Flying in a V formation, the black-faced geese swerved with the wind, trying to keep ahead of the winter cold that was coming from the north.

"See them geese?" Grizzly said. "They're flyin' places I ain't never been. Like Mexico." He turned to Longknife. "If you learn to read, you could read 'bout Africa even. Learn where you're from."

Longknife considered the words. "I know how to read things like the wind. Can't learn that from reading," he said, trying to follow the tracks.

"It's all in books," Grizzly said, then stopped and looked down. "And you can't read signs either. You 'bout missed this track."

"Looks like they *are* headin' towards Fort Henderson," Longknife said.

"I told you that," Grizzly said.

"How come you're always such a know-it-all?" Longknife complained. "Just 'cause you had some fancy-pants reporter write a yarn 'bout you, don't make you king of the mountain."

"If you'd learn to read, you'd see 'bout the things I've done," Grizzly said.

"Guess I'll never know then," Longknife sighed, "'cause I'm sure too old to go sittin' with a bunch of snot-nosed kids in a one-room schoolhouse."

"Never too old to learn," Grizzly said. "And I'm gonna learn you this now."

"What?"

"Watch where you step," he grinned, grabbing Longknife's arm to keep him from putting his foot down into Ben Franklin's fresh bear droppings.

"Thanks, don't need my moccasins stinkin' like that." Longknife looked in the direction they were headed and smiled. "I know a nice black family that lives up this way. Got them a pack of kids. They'll feed us for sure."

Grizzly looked at the tracks. *That's if Claw doesn't find 'em first.*

CHAPTER FOURTEEN

Three Children

Some three hours walk away, Claw Wyler and his band were skulking in a stand of trees watching an isolated settler's cabin. The mules with their pack saddles were tied in the ravine below.

The only sounds were from the three little children who sat on the rocks in front of the cabin. They looked dirty and hungry, but Claw didn't think much of it.

"Their parents got to be 'round here somewhere," Trapper whispered.

"Keep lookin'," Claw said softly. He wanted to kidnap the children and give them to Bear Robe to make up for the twenty bear skins they were short. "Thought there'd be a lot more," he said, looking at the kids. Something seemed wrong.

"Snake Indians will have fun with them two," Trapper whispered, watching the two girls draw stick men in the dust.

"Quiet," Claw said. "Their folks got to be around."

"Someone's comin' out," Claw whispered. A bearded old black man stepped out from the small wooden cabin.

"No one hurt the younguns," Claw warned, lifting his rifle.

"Let me shoot him," Trapper whispered, looking down at the elderly man.

Trapper raised his gun but Thunder pushed it down. "He's mine," the Crow whispered, taking the ironwood bow from his back. In his hands, the bow he'd smoothed with animal brains to make it pliable was a powerful weapon—one he liked to use when he intended to take a scalp.

His shafts were made from tough ash wood and could enter and exit the fattest war-horse of the flatland Indians. The arrow he took in his hand was grooved from feather to head, so that the blood of his enemy could flow easier.

The wild turkey feathers stood out, waiting to keep the arrow accurate in its flight. In front of the feathers, the Crow band's colors stood out, as well as Thunder's personal crest. The two other Crows watched silently as Thunder turned the bow horizontally, to match the horizontal plane of the old man's ribs.

"Don't miss," Trapper chuckled.

"I won't," Thunder whispered, letting the arrow fly. The silent blade of death spun through the air, entering the old man's chest.

"You got him," Trapper said, cocking his rifle.

Before the children's screams had left their mouths, the Indians had the two girls and the boy in their arms.

"The scalp is mine," Thunder said, looking down at the old man, keeping away the other Crows who wanted to add to their trophies. Thunder wanted it for the scalp dance when he returned to Bear Robe. He'd paint the skin side half red and half black and suspend it from his lodge pole.

Then they heard a roar as the big ghost bear came charging down the ridge after them. "What the...!" Claw shouted. The hunters had become the hunted.

The pack mules spooked and took off but they couldn't go far because they were all tied together. The bear attacked one of the Crows who had been traveling with Claw, breaking his neck with its paw. Thunder and the two Crows who had been left with the pack mules backed away.

"Let's get out of here," Trapper yelled.

"What 'bout the kids?" Claw asked.

"What 'bout 'em?" Trapper said, pointing his gun at the bear as he backed away. "Can't kill this bear. It ain't normal."

Thunder and the two Crows followed behind, leaving Claw to fight the bear alone. The grizzly charged. Claw ducked the swing of its paw, then followed the retreating Trapper.

The old man lay against the cabin, holding onto the arrow that had gone through his chest. The big bear backed off, then stood in the bushes between the children and the path that Claw and his men had taken. The three children wailed next to their grandfather, having already lost their parents to the cholera.

A hundred yards away, Claw and his men regrouped. "We got to find some children or women before the snows come."

"We'll find some more, don't worry," Thunder said, looking around to see if the bear had followed them. They all figured that the bear would eat the children.

"Like around Fort Henderson?" Trapper asked, grinning. They'd stolen children before from settlements and Fort Henderson was the closest one around.

"More there to choose from," Claw nodded.

Hours later, Grizzly Adams and Longknife were on

the path to the cabin. Ben had gone ahead, rumbling through the underbrush. Longknife wanted to know everything about Grizzly's past, asking question after question.

"Why won't you tell me 'bout your folks? What you expect me to do, get my bones out and read the past? You did have folks, didn't you?"

Grizzly kept his eyes on the tracks they were following. "'Course I had folks."

"That's good," Longknife said, "'Cause I was startin' to worry that you were birthed by a grizzly, suckled by wolves, and raised by the meanest snake around."

Grizzly saw Freedom slowly circling overhead and knew that something was wrong. He turned, wanting Longknife to be quiet. But before he could say anything, he saw the look on Longknife's face. The ferrets that had been riding on his shoulders scampered back into the carry-sack.

"What's wrong?" Grizzly asked, gripping his rifle.

"Tu...tu...turn around," Longknife whispered, nodding with his head.

Grizzly slowly moved his leg, turning around so he'd be in a position to drop and shoot. Standing there, not twenty feet away, was the big bear with the two missing toes. Ben was standing behind it.

"So we meet again," Grizzly nodded, looking the bear in the eye.

The big grizzly swayed back and forth, pawing the air. Then it got down on all fours and slowly trudged forward.

"Run," Longknife whispered.

"Don't move," Grizzly muttered. "This bear could run you down in twenty feet."

Longknife stood in absolute fear as the bear came within swatting distance of Grizzly's head. Then it raised up on its hind legs, towering above the men. It looked at Longknife, then back into Adams' eyes.

"Nice bear," Longknife whispered to himself, trying to remember every prayer he'd ever heard his mother say.

But Grizzly just stared into the bear's eyes, like they were communicating without speaking. He had a way with animals, especially bears, that was unexplainable.

Then the bear got down and walked back up the slope and stopped. "She's trying to tell us somethin'," Grizzly said.

"Yeah, like turn around and leave," Longknife whispered.

"Come on, we gotta follow her," Grizzly said, lifting up his Kentucky rifle.

Longknife followed a few steps behind Grizzly muttering, "I hate this *we* stuff."

But over the rise, the big bear was nowhere to be seen. In a small clearing were two graves. Longknife looked at the markers showing they'd died of cholera. "They were my friends," he whispered.

"Sorry," Grizzly said.

"They were good people," Longknife whispered. "Wonder what happened to their kids and their grandpa?"

Ben pulled at Grizzly's fringe. "What is it?" The bear ran toward the cabin below.

"Come on," Longknife said, taking the lead. He saw the injured old man leaning against the cabin and cried out, "Who would do somethin' like that?" he said, running ahead.

It was what Grizzly Adams had feared. "Claw Wyler," he swore.

"You okay, Grandpa?" Longknife asked quietly. The old man was having trouble breathing.

But the old man could hardly talk. "Kids...get the kids."

"Where are they?" Longknife asked. He'd figured that they'd been taken, along with the parents.

"Under the house," the old man grunted, sweat glistening on his wrinkled, ebony forehead.

Longknife looked at Grizzly and whispered into his ear, "He's gonna die, ain't he?" Grizzly nodded. The arrow had been in too long.

"Do what you can," Longknife said.

Longknife went to look for the children while Grizzly tended the wound. Indian arrows were ingenious weapons, designed to kill. Indians shot for a fleshy part of the body, hoping to hit bone.

"Hold on, Grandpa," Grizzly whispered, looking at the shaft, trying to figure out what the arrowhead was shaped like. He knew by the feathers that it was Crow and hoped that it wasn't poisoned.

The dilemma was how to withdraw the arrow before the body temperature dissolved the glue, disconnecting the shaft. Grizzly knew that unless the arrow was taken out within a half hour, the injured person would most likely die. He knew that the arrow had been in far longer and didn't know how the old man had survived as long as he had.

The old black man pulled Grizzly toward him. "Kids," he gasped. He died before Grizzly could pull the arrow out.

"I'll carry him up to the knoll," Grizzly said. "You look for the younguns."

Grizzly carried the old man up to where the two graves were. Longknife crawled back out from under the cabin.

"Any kids under here?" he asked, pushing away the cobwebs.

"Find 'em?" Grizzly asked as he came back down.

"Not yet," Longknife said. "Just hope there ain't no rats or snakes down here."

As Grizzly started to look inside the cabin Longknife called out, "I found 'em!"

"Look here," he grinned. "I got one," he said, lifting out a cute little girl.

Grizzly couldn't help but smile, then got serious. "But the old man said kids."

"Hold your britches," Longknife said, reaching down. He brought up a second girl.

"What are we goin' to do with them?" Grizzly asked.

"Wait a second, there's one more," Longknife said, reaching back down. He brought out a pudgy little boy and sat him next to his sisters.

"That's all they had," Longknife said smiling, then frowned. "Think they're sick with the cholera?"

Grizzly thought, then shook his head. "If they didn't die when it passed through, they're probably all right."

The three children looked around. Grizzly leaned forward and the boy started to cry. "Come on, now," he soothed him, picking him up.

Longknife came up. "You're doin' good, Daddy."

"Do you know anyone 'round here who can take 'em in?"

Longknife thought, then shook his head. "Nearest black family I know is in..."

"I don't care what color family; family is family," Grizzly said, putting the boy down.

"Better be with his own kind. Hard 'nough in this white world as it is," Longknife said.

Grizzly tried to understand what he meant. Longknife added with a serious look on his face. "Black folks always got to remake theyselves to keep white folks happy. I thought I'd found freedom when I escaped, but sometimes I kind of feel like a prisoner in my own skin in this country."

A long moment of silence passed, then Longknife changed his tone, "But as I was sayin', there's a black family runs a stable, in Fort Henderson, and since we're headin' that way, why I figure..."

"No," Grizzly interrupted. "I ain't carryin' three kids through the woods. Too dangerous."

"Can't just leave 'em."

"Got to be another way," Grizzly said.

"I got an idea," Longknife brightened. "We could take 'em back to your cabin and..."

"No," Grizzly Adams said bluntly.

"Hold on now, hear me out. We could take 'em back there and we could bring up the Buffalo Girls to momma them and..."

"Let's take 'em to Fort Henderson," Grizzly said flatly.

"That's what I first told you."

They buried the old man up where the bodies of his son and daughter-in-law lay. Longknife took off his cap, and said a prayer, then held his arms up into the wind. "Take their souls back to Africa where they be free. Speak their names on the wind, touch their souls. Free them from the pain and suffering that was heaped upon them in bondage."

Then he looked at Grizzly and whispered, "Give me a moment with the kids here," he said, hugging them to his side. Grizzly and Ben walked back to the house.

An hour later, after they'd collected clothing for the children from the cabin, Grizzly Adams and Longknife set out through the woods. "Still think you're makin' a mistake not wantin' your little honeybee princess," Longknife said. Grizzly shook his head. "Clean her up, put some perfume on her, why, she'd be real nice."

Grizzly fluttered his lips. "You can put perfume on a pig and call her a princess, but she's still a pig."

"That ain't nice."

"Never said I was. Now quit tryin' to make me daddy to these kids." Grizzly carried the boy under his arm and Longknife carried the two sisters.

"Can't figure out why them Crows didn't take the kids," Longknife said.

"The bear protected 'em," Grizzly said.

"Just don't figure, a grizzly bear helpin' out folks."

"That's somethin' you'll never understand," Grizzly said. Then he saw the look on the little boy's face and held him at arm's length.

"If he pees on me, I'm gonna drop him," Grizzly grumbled. The boy started to cry.

"Could you try bein' nice?" Longknife asked.

Grizzly put the boy on his shoulder and he went to sleep. Longknife felt the bones in his pouch. "Bet if I played Bone Up right now, the future would show that if you just keep your bearded mouth shut, that youngun will stay asleep."

Grizzly sighed, shaking his head, and stepped into the lead. They walked along in silence, each deep in thought about the dangerous men they were seeking.

Trouble had come to Grizzly Adams' valley. Trouble of the worst kind. Bear hunters and a man bent on settling an old score. Poachers who killed for greed, a madman who killed for fun, cholera that was killing the settlers, and Claw Wyler, who wanted to kill Grizzly Adams and mutilate his bear, Ben Franklin.

All of that was on Grizzly's mind as they followed the tracks. But there was no turning back. The choice was to take the fight or run, and Grizzly Adams didn't run from a fight.

But he had no idea that his only relative, a boy named Cody Jackson Adams, was on an orphan train heading to Fort Henderson.

An orphan train full of Boston children that nobody wanted. Nobody, except for Claw Wyler and the Crow Indians.

And up in the woods, a big grizzly bear with two missing toes was on the hunt for Claw and his band of renegades.

CHAPTER FIFTEEN

Fort Henderson

Doc Watters had arranged for a group of orphan children to be sent to Fort Henderson as part of a large
wagon train coming to Oregon. Coming with the children was a supply of laudanum, enough, they hoped, to
keep the town healthy. Since the town's Methodist
minister had died from cholera and a Methodist minister named Rev. Brice was looking for a church out
West, Doc Watters had made a deal. If Brice got the
medicine, then the town would ask him to be the new
minister.

When he'd made the announcement after church the
congregation had broken down in tears. It was like a
weight had been lifted from their shoulders and there
was renewed hope for the town. They were getting
children, medicine, and a new minister.

A growing group of pioneers, farmers, and mer-
chants had gathered around a long-awaited broadsheet
being posted in front of the combination general store
and post office. News of any kind was of interest in the
isolated territories, and news of the orphan children that
Doc spoke about was especially sought after.

When word began spreading that the poster was
about the orphans, it seemed that every wagon was
parked, every apron laid aside, and every rocking chair
stopped on the porches, so people could crowd around
and read it.

Jessie Dillon, a pretty widow in her mid-thirties
whose husband and son had died from cholera the past
spring, watched the broadsheet being posted. As the

town's only schoolteacher and Doc Watters' volunteer helper, the headline caught her attention:

WANTED

HOMES FOR CHILDREN!

A company of homeless children from Boston will arrive by Orphan Train at FORT HENDER-SON, on or about Thanksgiving 1850.

These children are of various ages and of both sexes, having been thrown friendless upon the world by their parents dying of cholera. They come under the auspices of the Boston Children's Mission of Boston, Mass. They are well disciplined, having come from the various orphanages and are disease free.

The citizens of this community are asked to assist the agent in finding good homes for them. Persons taking these children must be recommended and be of good character. They must treat the children in every way as a member of the family, sending them to school, church, Sabbath school and properly clothe them until they are 17 years old.

BOSTON CHILDREN'S MISSION

Big Jake Price, a good-natured mountain of a man with a stutter, whose son was stolen during the summer in an Indian raid, looked at the poster, then back at a picture of his son which he had in his hand.

One of the other men nearby patted him on the back. "Still no word 'bout your boy?"

Big Jake shook his head and put the picture away. "N...n...no," he whispered, his large eyes welling with tears.

The man nodded sympathetically. "Best accept the fact that he ain't comin' back. Injuns don't ever give people back." He tapped the poster. "You need to get yourself another boy. Like one of these orphans. Don't you think that's right, Mrs. Dillon?"

Jessie Dillon smiled and nodded, sensing Big Jake's hurt. "These kids need good homes. Are you interested, Jake?"

"M...m...maybe," Big Jake said with a slow shrug of his massive shoulders.

"You ought to be," Jessie smiled. "You've got a lot of love to give in that big heart of yours."

Big Jake smiled. "What *you* want, J...J...Jessie? A boy or a girl?"

Though he was trying to be nice, the mention of a boy reminded her of the son she'd lost. She closed her eyes and took a breath, trying to keep from crying. "A boy I guess. To replace my Tommy."

Big Jake grinned. "Me t...t...too."

One of the farmers reading the poster turned and said, "You'll need a big kid to keep up with you."

Jack shook his head. "Me and the missus don't care much what kind of b...b...boy we get—heck any kind would do for us."

"Whoever gets you will be a lucky boy, Big Jake," Jessie smiled.

"And whoever gets you will be a l...l...lucky man, Jessie," Big Jake said. "You need to find yourself another husband. Woman shouldn't be a...a...a...alone in these parts."

"Shame they don't have Husband Trains comin' out this way," she joked.

"They're everywhere you look," Big Jake said, nodding to the men behind him.

Jessie turned to see a group of bad-toothed, scraggly, ugly trappers laughing as they walked to the bar. Jessie rolled her eyes. "I'm not *that* lonely yet," she said coyly, walking away.

Big Jake saw the curve of her ankle as the wind picked up her skirt, and turned away red-faced. He took out the picture of his son, looking one more time, then tapped the poster and walked away.

Jessie nodded and greeted the various neighbors she passed. The town was the link between producer and supplier, taking in raw goods for the products from back East and San Francisco.

She stopped by Doc Watters' office to see if he needed help, but he was in the back putting on his coat. "Got a whole load of what-ifs to inspect," Doc called out.

Jessie looked around and smiled. Doc's house was a combination home, office, and reception center. His medical shingle over the front door was formal, but inside he had French blankets hanging from a rope to hide his bed, a table filled with medical instruments and kitchen utensils and a boxes of fruit and vegetables stacked in the corner which he'd taken as trade for his services.

On the cook stove in the corner, a corncake was

warming. On the wall above was a deer head and a dusty rack of antlers. Josie was always amused by this eclectic office, never knowing what she'd find.

"Need any help?" she asked.

"I'll send for you if things get real busy," he said, grabbing the corncake in a cloth and heading out the door.

Jessie knew that Doc Watters was in for a busy day inspecting the wagonloads of farmers with goods to trade. She'd seen them lined up outside the makeshift gate. Oxen loads stood in line near the feed store. Hunters and trappers sat outside the general store with their loads of hides to trade for supplies.

It wasn't an overnight mining town, but was a town trying to grow. Though Fort Henderson was primitive by Eastern standards, it was taking on the style of town life. There was a doctor, a lawyer, a bank, a newspaper, and a half dozen stores. The town had been divided into lots and by agreement, property was donated to the Methodist church, Masonic Lodge, and a Catholic Church on the edge of town for the Mexican workers who'd pushed inland.

Jessie walked slowly back to her small clapboard house on the edge of town. When her husband and son had lived there, the house had never seemed big enough. Now by herself, it seemed too big, too empty and too lonely.

Turning up the oil lamp, she saw that the yellowed clay between the wallboards needed patching. Like the broken board on the steps and the cracked window, she missed the man she had grown so dependent on.

Oh Luke, why'd you have to go? Why couldn't you have survived so we'd grow old together? She missed his easy laugh and loving arms that had kept her spirits up through the hard times.

Being an independent woman in a mountain town was not easy. Miners, trappers, and traveling no-goods were the bane of single and widowed women. The church-going men were either married or too old to worry about.

She looked at her husband's picture and felt her eyes well up. "I miss you so much," she said, trying to block the memory of burying him in the town cemetery. Her son, who died soon after his father, had taken a big piece of her heart.

There were orphans coming to town, orphans who needed good homes, but she knew that single women would never be allowed to adopt one. In a land where women couldn't vote and could hardly own property, they were allowed to be mothers to their own children, but could not take in those without family.

"I'm a long way from Missouri," she sighed, trying to perk herself up. *Would I go back to Cape Girardeau if I could?* she wondered.

Her life in Missouri seemed part of someone else's life, not her own. The only thing that kept the loneliness from driving her crazy was the frontier school she taught. A crowded, noisy room full of boys, girls, and confusion.

Though children in the Sierras were not required to go to school, Jessie was proud of the effort the town made to educate their own. But the pay was low. Just six dollars a month when school was in session. Hardly enough to feed herself, let alone keep the house fixed up.

The minister had suggested she give up the house and move in with one of the school families but Jessie had refused, saying she'd make it. She looked into her egg-money box, knowing that the dollar and ten cents she had the night before had not grown any larger.

"What am I going to do?" she whispered, wanting to cry.

Then Doc Watters burst through the door. "I need your help," he said, his eyes wild with worry.

"What's wrong?" she asked, but from the look in his eyes, she knew.

"Cholera," he said. "A whole wagonload of it. And we ain't got no laudanum left," he confessed.

"Did they get past the gate?"

Doc shook his head. "They're camped out by the well out there. Kept their sick kids hidden from everyone. We caught 'em tryin' to bury two little boys down by the river. Now the sheriff wants to burn their wagon and send 'em packin'."

Jessie closed her eyes at the sadness of it all, but knew they had no choice. They had to protect the people in the town who weren't sick.

Doc coughed. "They'll be forced away but no tellin' if that disease is gonna spread through town again."

"Pray. That's all we can do now," she said. Doc nodded, knowing that if the medicine on the wagon train didn't get there, then the disease would sweep through the town, killing everyone.

CHAPTER SIXTEEN

The Letter

Inside the general store, Charlie Boyer, the town's postmaster, was sorting through the mail. Trappers, farmers, and what few miners were still in the area stood patiently, waiting to see if their names would be called, talking about the weather, crops, and cholera.

"Come on, Charlie," an old farmer complained. "I've been waitin' a year for word from my wife."

An old crippled man playing checkers in the back laughed. "Word is she left you."

The farmer glared. "Lucky you got that bum leg or I'd teach you a lesson."

"Anytime," the crippled man said. "Ain't much worse you can do to me than the Indians already done." His name was Claxton and he was the only survivor of an Indian attack on a wagon train ten years before.

When Big Jake came in, the talk centered around the wagon train of orphans that was coming. Charlie joined in, saying, "Doc said that he's got enough cholera medicine coming on the wagon train to keep us all healthy."

"Not a moment too soon," said a farmer. "Way I hear it, there's some sick ones at the gate tryin' to get in."

"Doc won't let 'em in," Charlie said.

"Might not let them in," the farmer said, "but can't keep the sickness out. Darn thing's like a ghost the way it jumps walls and rivers to kill you."

After the letters were distributed to those waiting, the rest were laid out on a long table. It was Charlie's custom to cubbyhole the letters for those that came in once or twice a year, like the mountain men who traveled beyond the edge of the frontier.

Then he stopped and looked at a letter. It was addressed to:

John "Grizzly" Capen Adams
Fort Henderson, California

"Always wondered what his real name was," Charlie grinned. He looked up and called out to the folks in the room, "Anybody know when Grizzly will be coming into town?"

The group of old men playing checkers by the stove just shrugged and muttered. "He'll be here when he gets here," chuckled a toothless old man. "You know how Grizzly Adams is."

"Don't think he owns a clock," another said.

"Or a calendar," laughed Claxton, the crippled man. "He probably don't even know what year it is."

A trapper had come in with a load of furs. "Saw him at the rendezvous. Heard 'bout his ghost bear too. Any truth to that?"

Charlie paused, then said, "Some say it's real, some say it's not."

"What you think?" the crippled man asked.

An old farmer began one of the local stories that had grown out of proportion. "I seen the grizzly paw print with the two missing toes once. It was a dark, full-moon night and I was over by the graveyard and..."

"And if I want to step in it I'll go to my barn," a rancher in the back said.

The postmaster shrugged, looking back at the envelope. "Letter says here, *Urgent Business*. Says so right on the envelope," he said, tossing it into a slot on the wall marked *Grizzly Adams*.

"If it's so dang urgent, why don't you open it?" the toothless old man asked.

"That's 'gainst the law," the postmaster said.

Claxton spat into the spittoon that sat next to his bad right leg. The leg was drawn up where the Indians had cut his Achilles tendon. "If it was me, why I'd read everyone's letters so I'd know what was going on."

"But you can't read," said the toothless old man.

"Would if I could," the crippled man shrugged.

Curiosity got the better of the postmaster, so when he got a break from tallying what the customers bought, he took the letter and went into the storage room. Looking around, he held it up next to a lantern and tried to read it. But the paper was thick.

"I always can read the others," he muttered, adjusting the glow of the lantern. Unable to decipher the writing, he looked around, saw that no one was looking, then carefully slit it open.

"Well I'll be," he whispered as he read the letter.

District Court
Boston, Massachusetts

Dear Mr. John "Grizzly" Capen Adams:

A twelve-year old boy named Cody Jackson Adams, from Medfield, Massachusetts, whose parents succumbed to the fever of the past spring, has been made a ward of the court.

We can find no living relatives, but the boy claims that you are his uncle. In hopes that you are that relative and that you are a good God-fearing married man with home, we are sending him on the Boston Children's Mission's Orphan Train to Fort Henderson.

If you want him, you may claim him. Otherwise, he will be given to a good family in the territory.

Yours very truly,

John Peters

John Peters
Judge

The postmaster whistled. "Imagine. Grizzly Adams tryin' to raise a boy in the woods. That'll be the day."

CHAPTER SEVENTEEN

Orphan Train

It had been a hard six months from Boston to the Sierras, and the orphan wagons moved slowly, seemingly hitting every rut and hole in the road. The sturdy Conestoga wagons, with their waterproof white dustcovers that flapped in the wind, plodded their way through the mountains.

They'd abandoned the oxen fifty miles outside of Fort Bridger, because they'd only been able to make five miles a day. Now with the three teams of mules that pulled each wagon, they were making ten miles a day from sunup to sundown.

The wagons were homes, forts, hospitals, school rooms—whatever was needed at the moment. And on this trip, the lead wagon had served as a courtroom and scaffold. An argument had lead to a murder and the guilty man was tried, convicted, and hung from the wagon tongue, which served in place of a hanging tree. The wagon master had ordered two men to point the wagon tongue skyward, and the accused was pushed off the driver's seat with a rope around his neck.

The bullwhackers who drove the wagons were on the lookout for Indians, since they'd seen burned-out wagons and shelters in the Nevadas. The scalped bodies and butchered families had scared everyone.

There were also the endless cholera and smallpox graves along the old pioneer trails. Besides the dysentery, which affected almost everyone, thirty people had died along the way before the orphan wagons split off to head alone to Fort Henderson.

It had been hard at first for everyone to not mark the gravesites with crosses and memorials of some kind. But in a wilderness land surrounded by wolves, Indians, and ground too hard to spend time digging, they'd settled for shallow trenches covered by rocks.

They also didn't want to mark the graves because the Indians would come and strip the bodies of their clothes. It was one of the main ways that cholera had spread among the Western tribes. They'd take their trophy clothing back to their villages, bringing along the deadly disease.

And if the Indians didn't find the graves, the wolves did. No bodies were safe. But there was no time to tend to the dead when the living were sick and dying. So the wagon train had pushed ahead, hoping to make it to the Oregons before the sickness struck again.

For the orphan children, it was ride from sadness, through sadness, to the unknown. They had all lost their parents to cholera and were being sent West to be raised by people they'd never met.

It was this uncertainty that kept them on edge, fighting among themselves. They'd heard exaggerated rumors about orphans being given to farmers as virtual slaves, made to work until they dropped, so no matter what the minister on the ride told them, they were all worried.

But one boy knew who was waiting for him. Though he'd never met the man who was his uncle nor had any confirmation that the man knew he was coming, Cody Jackson Adams, a twelve-year-old blond boy with an easy smile, was convinced that his famous uncle

Grizzly Adams was going to be waiting for him. This it made the other children jealous.

He'd been assigned a seat in a wagon with five other children, all dressed in tattered store-bought clothes that had been new when they'd left Boston. But after five months, there wasn't a seam, knee, or piece of clothing that hadn't been patched and repatched.

There had been a constant struggle to see who was the leader. The main contest was between Cody and a mean-spirited boy named Pete, who didn't believe that Grizzly Adams was Cody's uncle.

Two sisters stayed in a corner by themselves. A small red-headed boy nicknamed Runt bore the brunt of Pete's abuse. A pretty twelve-year-old girl named Penny sat opposite Cody. She'd been amused at the way Cody blushed each time he looked at her, figuring that he liked her.

The driver looked in through the flap at Cody. "You readin' that again?" he chuckled.

Cody shrugged, "Got nothin' else to do but read. Ain't nothin' to see except same ol' things out there." The adventure of crossing America in a wagon had worn off after the first hundred miles.

"Say," he smiled, tapping the driver on the back, "you wanna arm wrestle again when we make camp?"

"I might give you 'nother go-round," the bearded man laughed. Cody was the arm-wrestling champion of the children on the trip and had begun challenging the adults.

Cody looked back at his dime novel with its printed yellow cover. *I know he's waitin' for me*, Cody thought. Though the court had not received any letter back from Grizzly Adams, Cody was sure that his uncle was going to take him in and teach him to be a mountain man.

I bet he loves kids, Cody thought. *I bet he'll be tickled pink to teach me everythin' he knows 'bout the woods.*

Cody looked at the cover again:

Life of J.C. Adams

**Known as Grizzly Adams, Containing a
Truthful Account of his Bears, Fights with
Poachers, Hairbreadth Escapes in the
Rocky and Nevada Mountains and the
Wilds of the Pacific Northwest.**

He had spent hours staring at the lurid colored picture of Grizzly Adams fighting off a dozen men. *I'll bet he's got a whole army of men fightin' with him, takin' on bandits and savages.*

Cody began to read from his favorite chapter:

> *Grizzly Adams and his trusted bear, Ben Franklin, ran down the narrow mountain trail, trying to capture the thieves. "Halt or I'll shoot," Grizzly shouted, but the men kept going. Ben Franklin raced towards the edge of the cliff. "Don't, Ben!" Grizzly cried out. But Ben raced forward.*
>
> *If he made it to the other side, he'd be in*

front of the bad men. If he missed, Grizzly Adams' faithful bear would fall five hundred feet to his death on the rocks of the raging rapids below.

Pete was bored and wanted to cause trouble. Every time he saw Cody engrossed in the dime novel, he wanted to rip it apart. "Grizzly Adams ain't gonna be there," he teased.

"He is too."

"And he ain't your uncle," Pete sneered.

"He is so!" Cody said flatly.

It had been a long-running feud between them that had kept the wagon load of kids on edge. Pete laughed. "Ain't nobody gonna be there to greet you 'cept a mean old farmer."

"Grizzly Adams is my uncle!" Cody said loudly. "He'll be waitin' for me!"

"You're an orphan like the rest of us!" Pete snapped.

Runt, the small red-head, spoke up for Cody. "You're just jealous, Pete, 'cause Cody's got a relative."

"Shut up," Pete growled, shoving the smaller boy into the sideboards of the wagon.

"Leave him alone," Penny said.

"Stay outta this," Pete snapped. He looked at Runt and raised his fist. "Gonna learn you a little lesson, Runt."

Cody sprang forward and grabbed Pete's arm. "Leave Runt alone," Cody said. Pete struggled to pull away but Cody was stronger.

The wagon hit a pothole and the two boys bumped

heads. A fight broke out. Runt stood up on the back of the wagon, cheering like it was a boxing match. "Come on, Cody, pound him!"

Penny watched, hoping that Cody would win. She didn't like the way that Pete looked at her.

Pete rolled on top of Cody, hitting him in the jaw, but Cody was stronger and flipped the heavier boy over, pinning him down. "Now you listen to me, you bully," Cody said, catching his breath. "You keep off Runt."

Penny grinned. "Way to go, Cody. That'll show 'im."

Pete glared at her. "You're trash just like Cody."

Cody hit Pete in the jaw. "Don't you ever insult her again," he threatened, not wanting to look at Penny. He didn't want to start blushing.

Rev. Brice looked in from the back flap. "What's going on here?" he asked.

"He hit me," Pete moaned, holding his jaw.

Rev. Brice tried to push Cody off of Pete. "Leave him alone, Adams." He didn't like Cody's smugness at having a relative. It made him harder to control and not as weak and submissive as the other orphans, who were alone in the world.

Cody released Pete, who got to his knees whining, "Cody started it."

"I did not," Cody answered, but Pete kept whining.

"He's been pickin' on me all the way, you got to do somethin' 'bout him, Rev. Brice."

"Ain't so," Cody said.

Rev. Brice looked between them. He felt a kinship for Pete since he'd known his parents back in the ward.

"Did Cody start it?" he asked the other children.

Runt shook his head, then turned to Penny who shook hers. Dissatisfied, Rev. Brice looked at Pete who had tears in his eyes. "They don't like me! They all pick on me 'cause I want to be a minister like you."

Cody rolled his eyes but the minister caught him. "Did you start it or did Pete?" Cody wouldn't answer. He wouldn't tell on anyone, believing that you settle your own problems without tattling. Rev. Brice threw his arms up in frustration. "You're a wild ruffian like that uncle you claim." He looked at the children, shaking his head. "If you don't act any better, no one will want you, then what will you do, huh?" The two girls began to cry.

"Now look what you've done," Rev. Brice said to Cody.

"I didn't do nothin'."

"That's what you always say," Rev. Brice said, pulling him by the hair.

Cody wanted to cry out in pain but held his tongue. Penny watched, admiring the inner strength in the boy. Pete snickered behind his hand.

Outside the wagon, Rev. Brice looked at Cody, shaking his head. "For starting that fight, you've got to walk until we make camp at Squaw pass."

Runt looked out. "But that's 'bout seven miles, the driver said."

"So be it," Rev. Brice said. "Maybe it will teach this ruffian how to behave."

Runt, who knew that the fight had started because Cody had stood up for him, climbed out. "If he's walkin', then I'm walkin'."

"That's your choice," Rev. Brice said.

He stepped quickly around to the side and went ahead to his wagon thinking about his new church in Fort Henderson. He'd worked a deal with Doc Watters, arranging for the laudanum supply in exchange for taking over the Methodist Church. Since the town's minister had died from the fever, it was a fair exchange.

Penny looked out and smiled. "Thanks Cody."

"For what?" he asked, feeling his cheeks turn red.

Penny couldn't help but smile because Cody was so cute. "Thanks for defendin' my honor."

Cody tried to speak but couldn't find the words. He was crazy over the girl and had trouble taking his eyes off her. Just being in the same wagon with her day after day was making him lovesick.

As the wagon pulled ahead, Runt started skipping along in the dust like they were going to a picnic. "Tell me 'nother story 'bout your Uncle Grizzly," he said.

"Well," Cody began, "did I ever tell you the story 'bout the time my Uncle Grizzly Adams took on twenty-five savage Indians to save Ben Franklin's life?"

Runt nodded. He'd heard the dime novel chapter a dozen times, but wanted to hear it again. "Tell it slow this time."

"We got a lot of time to kill 'fore we make camp," Cody said, and began his story.

CHAPTER EIGHTEEN

Renegades Enter Fort Henderson

The mixed band of whites and Crows made quite a sight as they entered Fort Henderson. People on the streets stopped to stare at the wild-looking men, the Indians with scalps, and the pack mules loaded down with eighty bearskins.

The bear teeth and claws that hung from their necks matched the meanness of their eyes. Women hid their children's faces when Claw looked in their direction. No one was sure if they were friends or foes, and with the Indian raids that had been going on, most everyone kept their distance.

Claw Wyler and his men entered the town without stopping, pushing Doc Watters out of the way. They headed right down the center of town, eyeing the women and kids like they were looking at goods in a store.

"You lookin' to trade those skins here?" asked Josh Hewlett, owner of the feed store. He'd made money off bearskins before and saw a quick profit riding in.

"You stay away from these skins," Trapper growled, pointing his rifle. "These are already sold."

"To who?" Hewlett asked.

"Crows," said the old hunter sitting on the horse trough. It was Flash, who'd seen Trapper at the rendezvous.

"Do I know you, you old fart?" Trapper asked.

"Our paths have crossed," Flash said, "but we ain't never walked together."

"Keep goin'," Claw ordered.

Hewlett walked over to Flash as the men rode by. "What do Crows want all them bearskins for?"

Flash spit into the dust. "Think bear teeth and hides cure the sickness. Damn ignorant if you ask me."

Claw wondered why there were so few children. *The town was crawling with 'em before.* He stopped at the newspaper office as the editor came out. "Hey, newspaper man," Claw said.

"You talkin' to me?" Gordon Harris asked, trying to keep his composure at the sight of such a horrible face.

"Yeah, I'm talkin' to you," Claw growled. "Where are all the children?"

Harris shook his head. "Cholera took a dozen, real tragedy it was." Then he smiled. "But we got more comin' on the wagon train along with enough medicine to keep the town healthy."

Claw cocked his head. "Say what?"

"That's right," Harris bragged. "We got an orphan train comin' to Fort Henderson and a bag of laudanum."

"Laudanum? You got the cure comin'?" Claw said. The word caught his attention. Laudanum was worth its weight in gold five times over and it was just what he needed to bring to Bear Robe.

Harris smiled. "We all chipped in and got enough for Doc to be able to mix it up with camphor. It'll be a blessed day when it gets here."

"And not a day too soon," said an elderly church lady walking by. "There's a family down with the sickness in the old barn north of town."

Claw rode on, then dismounted and tied his horse up in front of the saloon. He gave the Indians money for drink, and took Trapper into the alley.

"If we get our hands on that medicine, we can make Bear Robe dance for us."

"Don't want him to dance," Trapper said. "Just want him to give me 'nough loot to make it 'til next summer without workin'."

"It's worth more than you'll ever know," Claw said. He headed back out onto the muddy street with Trapper following two steps behind.

Settlers stood to the side muttering and looking down when the mean, burly men cast glances at them. Jessie Dillon had gone to the small hotel to eat and came out just as the men walked by. She turned her head to avoid the smell of bear grease on the men.

Claw saw her squinch her nose and asked, "What's wrong, lady? Don't like the smell of real men?"

"Men or dead men?" she said, not giving them even a second glance.

Trapper laughed. "She don't like the stink of bear grease, Claw. Guess we need a bath 'fore she'll dance with us."

"I could dance on her without bathin'," Claw said, leering with his one good eye.

"If my husband were here, why he'd..."

Big Jake Price came up and stood beside Jessie. "Don't t...t...talk to her like that. Sh...sh...she's a widow lady."

Trapper spat, shaking his head. "Looks like we got ourselves a st...st...st..." It was obvious that Trapper was making fun of Big Jake's stutter. Trapper slapped his own face and spat out the word, "A...a... stutterer.

Ain't that right, big man?" He took off his bear cap and scratched where he'd been scalped.

Jessie felt embarrassed for her friend. "And it's obvious that we got ourselves someone who belongs in a barn," she said. "Now if you don't mind," she said, walking off, taking Big Jake by the arm.

Claw watched her go. "I like a woman who'll fight."

Trapper grinned, enjoying the way they'd upset Jessie. "Not me," he said, watching her walking away.

Big Jake looked back, then said quietly to Jessie, "That was Cl...Cl...Claw Wyler," he whispered, as if everyone in the world knew the name.

"Who?" asked Jessie.

"Claw Wyler...the man Grizzly Adams run out of these p...p...parts."

"Looked more like a nightmare," Jessie shrugged. "Did you see his face? It's enough to scare you to death."

"Heard that the ghost bear did that to him," Jake said.

"Now, Jake," Jessie grinned, "don't start talking about that ghost bear again. It's just so much nonsense, if you ask me."

"I've seen the track with the two missing toes," he nodded.

"Ah huh, and I've seen the cow jump over the moon," she smiled, shaking her head.

Claw opened the door of the general store. He and Trapper entered, followed by Thunder and the two braves. While the merchant watched helplessly they proceeded to sample food and drink at will, without asking or paying for any of it.

The old men playing checkers stopped their game. Thunder knocked their board over. Claxton, the crippled man, reached out to grab the Indian's wrist, but Thunder took him by the hair and glared into his face.

He saw the design of the cut marks on the man's arms and knew he'd been tortured by Indians. "I see that the Utes already cut you," he whispered. "They should have finished it."

"Quit eatin' that candy," Charlie Boyer shouted out. He couldn't take it anymore, watching them steal his goods.

"You gonna stop me?" Trapper asked, taking off his bear cap to show his scalp scar. It was an effective way to shut most people up. Boyer just stared, slack-jawed. "Thought so," Trapper said, putting his cap back on. He reached into a jar of candy and loaded up his pockets.

A hunter, sitting on a pile of furs he'd brought to trade, stood up to defend Boyer, but Trapper's knife was out and up against his neck before he could say anything. "Don't even think 'bout helpin', or I'll skin you like them furs."

Claw came up and looked the mountain man in the eyes. "You seen Grizzly Adams?" he asked, but the man just shook his head. Claw spun around and shouted out to the store. "Has anyone here seen Grizzly Adams recently?"

He walked over to Boyer, who was holding a letter in his hand which he'd been about to hand over to a farmer. "I'm askin' you now," Claw said quietly. "You seen Grizzly Adams?"

The postmaster shook his head. Trapper came up and put his knife to the man's throat, digging deeply into his neck. "If the cat ain't got your tongue, then I'm gonna cut it out if you don't speak up...you hear me?" he said, drawing blood.

"Ain't seen him around," Boyer blurted out.

Trapper walked behind the counter and looked at the mail slots. "Looks like you got one for 'bout everyone in the territory, don't ya'?" Boyer nodded.

Trapper looked over at the letters in the slots. "Here's one for Grizzly Adams," he says, holding it up for Claw to see.

The postmaster reached up to grab it. "That's property of the..." Trapper put the knife back to his neck.

Claw took the letter and said in a slow, deep voice. "It's property of *me*."

Everyone in the room was watching. Claw knew the effect his face had on people and used it to his advantage. "You boys be good and I won't have to kill you," he said, opening the letter.

"What's it say?" Trapper asked.

Claw read it, smiling and nodding. "Looks like Grizzly Adams' got hisself a nephew comin' on the wagon train that newspaper man was speakin' 'bout."

"Nephew? Grizzly Adams?" Trapper asked, like it was the most astounding thing he'd ever heard. A buzz started among the men in the room who were following the conversation.

"Shut up!" Claw screamed out. He looked at a map that was tacked on the wall and traced the only path possible that the wagon's could be following.

"When's them wagons gettin' here?" he asked.

Boyer coughed. "Supposed to arrive here 'bout Thanksgivin'."

"When's Thanksgivin'?" Claw asked. He hadn't looked at a calendar for months, relying on the seasons as his guide.

Boyer said. "Couple days."

Claw looked around the room. "Anyone heard anything about a group of wagons comin' up the south trail?" It was the only way Claw figured they could come in.

The hunter sitting on his skins spoke up. "Heard 'bout some four-five wagons comin' this way."

"How far away?" Trapper said, impatient with the slowness of the conversation.

"Heard they was 'bout ten days away from here."

"And when was that?" Trapper asked, raising his voice.

"That was at the rendezvous which was..."

Trapper cut him off and figured on his fingers, then he turned to Claw. "That means those wagons are 'bout a day or so off."

Claw looked at the hunter. "Were they bein' pulled by mules or oxen?"

"Mules," the man said, feeling bad for getting involved.

Claw began figuring. Oxen pulled slow and didn't do more than five miles a day on flat land. Mules didn't travel more than ten miles when it was low land. These wagons were pulling high, which would slow the mules down, so he calculated that the wagons were about ten to twenty miles southeast.

Trapper walked over and bent his head toward Claw's. "Forget 'bout the kids," he whispered. "Bear Robe's already got ten or twelve of 'em to trade to the Snake River tribe. What you want is the fever medicine."

Charlie Boyer pretended not to listen but he'd heard every word. Now he knew where the town's kidnapped children were.

"I want the medicine," Claw grinned, "and one kid on that wagon train." Claw clutched the letter. "This one's special. It'll bring Grizzly Adams right to me...on my terms."

Trapper looked over and caught Boyer listening. "What you think you're doin'?" he asked, slapping the man down with one blow.

Claw walked over to the window and looked out. He saw Jessie Dillon across the street. Claw picked Boyer up and dragged him to the window. "Who's that spunky woman?"

Boyar looked out, then closed his eyes as if he were signing her death warrant. "That's Jessie Dillon."

Claw let the collar go, unable to take his eyes off the woman. It reminded him of the type of women he had always wanted to have before the bear had left his face so bad that no woman could look at him without flinching. "She married?"

Boyer shook his head. Trapper kicked him from behind. "Speak up!" he ordered, brandishing his knife.

"Widow...she's a widow woman," Charlie Boyer

stammered. "Fever took her husband and boy."

"Means she's a might lonely by now," Trapper said, patting Claw on the back.

Claw shrugged off his hand and watched Jessie turn into the doctor's house. "Might just want to hibernate with her for the winter," Claw leered, "after I get Grizzly Adams."

He looked at Trapper and a knowing glance passed between them. "Let's go," Claw said. "We got an orphan train to meet." He dropped the letter as he left the store. Outside, he sent the two Crows in charge of the pack mules to take the skins to Bear Robe.

"Tell him that we're gonna go get him a special gift for his vision," Claw grinned.

"Don't play games," Trapper complained. He looked at the Indians and said, "You tell the medicine man that we're gonna bring him some kids."

"And medicine," Claw added.

But Trapper shook his head. "Surprise him with that. He's already tryin' to fight off the white man's disease. He'll just think it's poison unless Thunder here explains it."

"That right, Thunder?" Claw asked.

The Indian nodded, then spoke in the Crow's language to the others, telling them that when he and Trapper came back, that he would kill Trapper. The two Crows grunted.

"And tell them to send us some braves to meet us along the East Trail near Squaw Pass," Claw said, pointing off in the distance. "Let's go," he said. He saddled up and rode out of town, followed by Trapper and Thunder. They took the southeast path, galloping through the woods heading toward where Claw figured the wagon train would be.

If he figured right, they were on a collision course that would take them to the wagon train and the children, the medicine, and the nephew of Grizzly Adams.

The thought of having Grizzly's nephew made Claw shiver. *I'll force him to come to me, to trade for the kid's life. Then I'll kill Grizzly, his bear, and the kid. I'll wipe 'em all out.*

For the moment he'd forgotten about the big grizzly bear with the two missing toes. But the bear hadn't forgotten about him. It watched from the ridges above, taking the rock trails which were shorter, staying near Claw and the two other renegades.

Back at the fort, inside the store, the men were discussing what Charlie had overheard. When Big Jake heard what had been said about Bear Robe and the dozen stolen children, he could hardly hold the picture of his kidnapped boy without weeping. "Please, God," he whispered, "bring my boy back to me."

Fifteen miles away, hidden in a ravine, Bear Robe was exhorting his braves to dance faster. Bearskins were hung in a circle around the fire. Two men and a woman were laying on the ground, burning up with fever.

"Bring more bear teeth and claws," the medicine man ordered.

The symbols and pictures on the lodges behind them

were of bears and their hunts. A recently killed bear was spread-eagled between two large poles. Two squaws were cleaning it.

They had done everything according to the vision, but the disease had come back again. If it didn't stop now, they could go no further west because Bear Robe had heard from the Modoc tribe that the land dropped off into a big lake just beyond the Sierras.

A procession of braves carrying scalps suspended from sticks came in dancing. Bear Robe knew that the three people were going to die. That the medicine from the bear skins and teeth wasn't enough. That even the scalp dance did no good.

But in his second vision since coming to the Sierras, he'd dreamed of sacrificing children—of killing them to save the soul of his tribe from the dreaded white man's diseases.

We've come so far, he thought, watching his dancing followers. *We cannot end our days so far from home. I must have children, like the vision said. Their blood will save us.*

From the pen behind him, a dozen small faces stared out: One of them was Big Jake's son. When the pack mules arrived with Claw's skins, Bear Robe sent a small party of braves out to join them at Squaw Pass.

CHAPTER NINETEEN

Possum Hunters

"What kind of family you want to take you?" Runt asked as they walked along in the dust behind the wagons.

Cody shrugged. "I told you, my Uncle Grizzly Adams is gonna be waitin' for me. What kind of family you want to take you?"

Runt thought for a moment, then grinned. "I just want someone who wants kids."

"Don't you want 'em to be rich or have a big farm?"

"Naw," Runt said, "I just want 'em to want me. That's all."

Runt thought about Cody's uncle for a moment, then asked, "You ever met your uncle?" Cody shook his head. "You ever get a letter writ from him?" Again Cody shook his head. "Then how do you know he even knows you're comin'?"

"'Cause the Judge sent him a letter and..."

Runt sighed. "'Member all them burned wagons we saw on the prairie. What if one of them was carryin' the letter to your uncle? Then he wouldn't know nothin' 'bout you comin'."

"He'll be there," Cody said confidently.

By the time they reached camp, Rev. Brice had already made the children do their chores and say grace for supper. Cody and Runt came up to where the food line was, but the minister turned them away.

"You didn't do your chores."

"We just got here," Cody said. "I'll do double tomorrow."

Rev. Brice frowned. "You know my rules. No work, no food. It teaches you responsibility and builds character."

"Builds skeletons," Runt mumbled.

"What did you say?" Rev. Brice asked.

Cody stepped in to cover for his smaller friend. "He just said he was hungry, that's all."

"You'll just have to wait until breakfast for your food," the minister said, walking away.

Pete stuck his tongue out. "Hope you starve to death."

"Don't bet on it," Cody said.

Pete grinned. "You've been readin' 'bout that make-believe mountain man so much, why don't you just go and trap yourself dinner?"

"Maybe I will." Cody said.

Runt thought he was serious. "I once had possum and taters at my aunt's house. They hunted the possum and..."

"Hush now," Cody said. He'd never hunted in his life. All his knowledge about the woods and Indians had come from the dime novel and his overactive imagination. Living in the city had not given him the chance to experience anything like their present surroundings.

Penny had gone through the food line ahead and walked by Cody with something in her apron. She nodded towards the side of the wagon and Cody walked over.

"Here," she said, handing him a roll. "You want some of this?" she asked, showing him the food on her plate.

"You've done enough already," Cody said. The way she looked at him made him blush again.

Pete saw Cody slip the roll in his pocket and went and told Rev. Brice. "Give it to me," the minister said to Cody.

"Give what?"

"The roll that you're not supposed to have."

Cody looked at him, then took the roll from his pocket. Rev. Brice looked at Pete and handed it to him. "That's your reward," he smiled, walking away.

Pete grinned and stuck his tongue out. He didn't see Runt's foot go out and he tumbled down with his face landing in the food. All the kids laughed so loud that Rev. Brice came trotting back over.

"Now what's wrong?" he asked in exasperation.

Pete sat up, wiping the food from his face. "Runt tripped me."

"No he didn't," Cody said, "I did."

Penny knew that Cody was defending his smaller friend and admired him all the more. Runt started to argue, but a look from Cody silenced him.

Rev. Brice looked between the boys, then said, "You're both guilty."

"Whip 'em," Pete said.

"No," Rev. Brice frowned. "I won't make a martyr of this boy," he said, looking Cody in the face. Then he turned to Penny. "For sneaking a roll to Cody, you're to sleep in the supply wagon tonight."

That was a punishment the kids hated because there were always field mice running around in it.

Then he looked at Cody and Runt. "And you two

boys, for picking on Pete, you're to go sleep in the woods up on the knoll," he said, pointing up toward the darkening hill.

"By ourselves?" Runt gasped.

"What's wrong?" Pete sneered. "Don't Cody know 'bout campin'?"

"Come on, Runt," Cody said. "Sleepin' up there will be better than sleepin' 'round this baby," he said, smiling at Pete. As they walked away, Penny winked at Cody, which made him blush.

They sat on the hill, watching the camp activity. Runt turned to Cody and said, "Thanks for stickin' up for me."

Cody shrugged. "You stuck up for me. Just like wilderness brothers."

Cody explained how Grizzly Adams had become a wilderness brother with an Indian through a simple grasping of hands and a pledge to protect each other. "I read it all in the book," Cody said proudly.

"I...I...I'd like to be your brother," Runt said, looking down.

Cody reached out and took Runt's hand. He repeated the pledge that Grizzly had said to the Indian. It ended with "and we'll always be brothers forever."

"Forever," Runt whispered, squeezing Cody's hand like he was absorbing the family he never had.

An hour later, as the sun was going down, Runt's stomach began to rumble. He looked down on the wagons as the others were preparing for the night, wishing he hadn't missed dinner.

He looked over at Cody who was looking at his dime

novel. "You hungry?"

"Yup."

Runt waited for more but Cody wasn't talking, so he said, "Got anythin' to eat?"

"Nope."

"Got any ideas on what we can eat?"

Cody tapped the page with his finger and looked up. "We're gonna have ourselves possums for dinner."

"Possums? Where do they live?"

"You said you'd eaten some and..." But Runt was shaking his head.

"But they were just on the plate. I didn't know if they fished for 'em or what."

Cody showed him the page in the dime novel where Grizzly Adams hunted enough possum to feed a starving town of settlers.

"Lookee here," he smiled. "I figure we'll catch ourselves a dozen possums or so and just lay up here after we eat them and burp ourselves to sleep."

"You gonna cook 'em or eat 'em raw?"

Cody took a quick look back in the book and found the right page. "Says here that you cook 'em."

"Ever skinned or cleaned out an animal?" Runt asked.

"Nope," Cody said, standing up, "but I'm sure it won't be a problem. Can't be more difficult than eatin' a cooked chicken."

Runt looked at Cody. "What does a possum look like?"

Cody looked back through the small book. "Says here that it's got a long tail and a pink nose with a lot of teeth."

"Sounds like a rat," Runt shivered, "and I ain't eatin' no rat."

"You already ate a possum you said."

"Didn't look like no rat. Was sittin' on a plate, cut up like a chicken breast. How the heck do I know what it looks like."

Then Cody beamed. "Lookee here," he said triumphantly. He found a small drawing in the book of Grizzly Adams holding a dozen possum. "This must be it."

Runt stared at the page. "Still think it looks like a rat. Kind o' lost my appetite."

"You'll get hungry again. Come on," Cody said, going off on his first hunt.

It took the boys a while to find a possum in a tree, because in the shadows, every lump or squirrel's nest looked right. Finally, Cody spotted one and chased it up a pine tree. He watched the possum scurry up to the top, climbing out along the tallest branch.

Cody looked at Runt and said, "Now you climb on up there and bring it down."

"Me, why me?"

Cody pointed up. "See that branch up there. It takes a small person to climb out without the branch breakin' off." He pushed Runt forward. "Now you shinny up there and throw 'im down to me."

Runt folded his arms. "Don't want to."

"Why? You scared?"

Runt nodded. "I ain't never touched a possum. What if it bites my hand off?"

"It's just a possum, it ain't a mountain lion."

"It's got teeth, don't it?"

Cody thought for a moment, then nodded. "Guess so. All animals got teeth."

"So if it's got teeth, it'll bite." Runt looked up the tree. "You go up and get it and I'll cook it." Both had decided that cooking was the safest choice although neither had addressed the fact that they didn't have any coals.

Cody took the challenge and shinnied up the tree. With the sun going down, it was very dark near the top, and the possum's glowing eyes made it all the more frightening.

At the top of the tree, Cody reached out for the possum but it bit his thumb hard. "Ouch!" he screamed.

"You okay?" Runt called out from below.

"Yeah, but I'm about to prove who's the hunter up here," he said. Holding onto the branch with his legs, Cody raised both hands, distracted the possum with one hand while grabbing it by the tail with the other.

The possum spun around, trying to bite him and Cody slipped sideways on the branch. "Oh no," he whispered, looking down. Then with a loud whooping shout, Cody swung the possum around his head and tossed him from the tree. Runt saw it coming and ran for cover. Neither saw that the possum bounced gently down the thick pine boughs and landed on a pile of pine needles.

"Get him and cook it up," Cody said, spitting on his thumb to clean off the blood. He started back down the tree.

Runt walked over to where the possum was laying. It was playing dead, which is something possums can do for hours when they sense danger.

Runt picked it up like it was a loaf of bread and stuck it under his arm. "Come on down," he shouted triumphantly to Cody.

The first thing Cody did when he got down the tree was wash his finger in the small stream behind them. Then he walked over to Runt who was holding the possum. "That's enough for a feast," he said, feeling like a great hunter.

"I can already taste it," Runt smiled, licking his lips.

Then it dawned on them that they needed to start a fire. "You know how to make one?" Runt asked.

Cody opened up the dime novel and flipped through the pages. "My uncle just always seems to have a fire goin'. It don't say nothin' 'bout how you get the flame, only tells what he cooks on the flame."

"That don't do us much good," Runt said, holding up the possum. "And I ain't eating it raw."

Cody looked down at the wagons below. "Guess we'll just have to go get us some cookin' coals."

"But Rev. Brice told us to stay up here 'til morning," Runt exclaimed.

"And if ol' Rev. Brice told you to eat that possum raw, would you do it?" Runt didn't hesitate, he shook his head no. "That's what I thought," Cody said. "Now let's go get ourselves some cookin' coals."

The boys used the shadows of the approaching night to sneak down to the camp. Runt carried the possum under his arm like it was a loaf of bread, oblivious to the fact that it was very, very much alive.

Penny spied them coming and caught Cody's attention. *Watch out*, she mouthed, pointing behind the wagon. Cody saw that Rev. Brice was sitting on a rock, reading his Bible.

Thanks, Cody mouthed, and Penny winked.

The two boys crept over to the wagon that fronted the cooking fire that was being put up until morning. Cody found a tin cup and was preparing to kick a coal from the fire when Pete spotted them.

"What are you doing down here?" he asked, looking at Runt and Cody. Then he saw what was in Runt's arms and grabbed it. "And what's this?" he asked, pulling the possum into his wagon.

Pete held it up and eyeballed it. "You got yourselves somethin' to eat, don't cha?" he said, sniffing it.

The possum opened its mouth and bit down on Pete's nose so hard that blood splurted everywhere. Pete screamed out in pain so loud that it sounded like he was being scalped alive by Indians.

"Get it off me!" he screamed, jumping from the wagon. He ran through the camp with the possum clamped onto his nose. He climbed into the other kids' wagon and the scared animal let go.

The other kids saw it. One of the boys shouted, "It's a monster rat!" and chaos broke out. The wagon drivers came running over with their rifles, thinking it was Indians attacking and no one saw the possum slink away into the night.

By the time things had settled down, Cody and Runt had been sent back up to the woods under no uncertain orders to not come back until morning. Pete sat moaning in the wagon, holding his bloody nose.

Penny watched the two boys trudge off, wishing she was with them. She pushed aside the medicine satchel that was marked: *Deliver to Doc Watters, Fort Henderson.* She had no idea that the fate of the entire town rested on the contents of that bag.

As they sat in the dark, waiting for the stars to come out, Runt looked over to Cody and asked, "You sweet on Penny?"

Cody started to deny it, then stopped. "Not sure what you're supposed to feel. Just feel like I like her."

"You're sweet on her," Runt grinned, then he turned serious. "Would you rather kiss a girl or eat a worm?"

Cody looked over like his friend was crazy. "That's not much of a choice."

Then Runt surprised him. "Me, why, I'd rather kiss a girl. Might puke if I ate a worm." They both laughed, which dispelled the lonely feeling that was coming on with the darkness.

"How come the possum didn't die when you flung it down?" Runt asked.

Cody shrugged. "Guess he was lucky, that's all. In my book it says they play possum and pretend they're dead. Grizzly Adams said he used that trick once when he was wounded to keep a bunch of bandits from killin' him."

"He did?" Runt exclaimed.

"He sure did," Cody said proudly. "Why, my uncle is the bravest, smartest man in the world."

"Wish I had an Uncle Grizzly," Runt whispered

looking away.

Cody was quiet for a moment, embarrassed that he'd bragged so much. He looked at the smaller boy who was now his friend and put his arm around him. "How'd you ever get the name Runt?"

The redheaded boy shook his head. "Dunno. The doctor said that I looked like the runt of ma's litter and it just kinda stuck."

The mention of Runt's dead mother made both boys think of the life they'd left behind—of the life they'd never have again.

"You miss your ma?" Runt asked.

"Sure. Don't you miss yours?"

"Sometimes when I think 'bout her, it's like it's part of a dream. Like she never existed. That it's all in my mind."

"What 'bout your pa?" Cody asked.

"Never knew him. He died 'fore I was born."

Cody thought for a moment, then nodded. "It all seems so far away. Boston was never anything like this."

"We're a long way from Boston, ain't we, Cody?"

"Too far to ever go back," Cody nodded.

On a small hill in the wilderness, miles from the nearest town, the two boys sat watching the moon come up. They didn't know a thing about surviving in the woods, about guns, or about Indians.

Everything Cody knew had come from reading the dime novel, which had been written by an Eastern tenderfoot writer prone to exaggeration. But even if they both had camped, hunted, and shot guns before, it wouldn't have helped them against Claw Wyler and his men, who had found the wagon camp.

It also wouldn't have helped them against the massive grizzly bear with the two missing toes who was hiding in the woods, watching it all, waiting to strike again.

"Want to go get 'em now?" Trapper asked, looking at the wagon drivers with rifles who were standing guard.

"No, we'll go in at dawn when they ain't so ready," Claw said. He looked to the northeast, where he figured Grizzly Adams was and thought, *I'll be killin' you soon, Adams. I'll have the revenge I've been waitin' on.*

Then a shiver raced through him. For a moment Claw thought the big bear was coming at him again, ripping at his face. Night sweats broke out and he shivered. Then the feeling passed. *Guess I'm just spooked, that's all*, Claw thought, not knowing that what he feared most was watching him from the woods above.

CHAPTER TWENTY

Room for Two

It was dark when Grizzly, Longknife, Ben, and the three black children arrived at Fort Henderson. They were let in without question because they kept quiet about the children's parents dying of the dreaded disease.

Longknife looked around the deserted streets, depressed. "Where's all the action?"

"This town's 'bout rolled up for the night," Grizzly said. "Now where's that family you said would take these kids?"

They walked down Main Street until they got to the stable. Longknife greeted his friends and took the kids inside, leaving Grizzly and Ben outside.

Doc Watters came up with Jessie Dillon. They were making the rounds of those that hadn't been feeling well, checking on who might have the sickness. "Heard you were in town, Adams," Doc said. "See you got your bear with you."

"Hey, Doc," Grizzly smiled, then turned to Jessie. "Evenin', m'am." He felt something in his heart that he hadn't felt in years. Jessie looked down, blushing.

Doc saw the look that passed between them. "This is Jessie Dillon. She's the prettiest schoolmarm and the best nurse between St. Louis and San Francisco."

"I've heard of you, Mr. Adams," Jessie said, extending her hand, "and your bear." Ben sat up, pawing at the air in a friendly manner.

"Wish I'd heard of you, Mrs. Dillon," Grizzly smiled.

Doc started to correct him but stopped. "We're just

comin' back in from our rounds. Terrible thing this cholera, ain't it?"

Grizzly nodded. "Found a lot of graves along the trail east of here. Couple cabins burned out."

"Indians?" Jessie asked.

"Saw signs that Crows have been around. Found one old man nearly dead with a Crow arrow in him."

"Scalped?" Doc asked. Grizzly shook his head. "That's strange."

"Guess somethin' stopped 'em," Grizzly said.

Jessie turned to Doc. "Didn't you say those were Crow Indians who came through town today?" That caught Grizzly's attention.

Doc nodded. "Yup. Some bad-lookin' whites and Crows with a string of pack mules loaded down with bearskins."

"One's face was so horrible," Jessie said, closing her eyes at the thought.

"Face?" Grizzly said.

"Looked like he was from Hell itself," Doc said.

"Terribly scarred up," Jessie added.

"Did he say his name?" Grizzly asked.

"Some of the hunters 'round here recognized him. Said his name is Claw Wyler," Doc said. Grizzly set his jaw at the name. "Also heard him say somethin' 'bout a Crow medicine man who's got stolen children."

Jessie looked at Grizzly. "We've lost a dozen of our children in Indian raids, but no one's been able to find where the Indians took 'em."

"We were hopin' that you could help," Doc said. "Charlie heard one of 'em say something about a Crow camp in the canyon."

"We're headin' out tomorrow at dawn," Grizzly said. "We're huntin' Claw Wyler and his band. Maybe they'll lead us to this Crow camp."

"And we were also hopin' that you could make sure that the orphan train gets here safely," Doc said.

"Orphan train? Don't know anythin' about it," Grizzly said.

Doc told him about the orphans coming and the medicine that the town desperately needed. Grizzly knew that Claw was hunting bearskins for the Crows who used them to ward off the sickness. "That laudanum's more valuable than gold," Grizzly said.

"Men will kill for it," Doc said, sighing.

Jessie looked at Doc, waiting for him to say more. Finally he relented. "And ol' Charlie Boyer the postmaster said that there's a letter to you over there and..."

"And what?" Grizzly asked.

"And Claw Wyler read it," Jessie said.

"And?" Grizzly said.

"And you better read it yourself," Doc said. He took Jessie by the arm. "We'll be over at the hotel eatin' if you want to join us."

Grizzly looked into the stable where the black couple were hugging the three small children he and Longknife had rescued. "Longknife, I'm gonna be over at the general store."

"I'll meet you at the hotel," Longknife said, then turned back to the couple and continued bragging. "As I was sayin', after I fought off twenty-three bandits, I managed to run through a storm of flaming Injun' arrows and grabbed these three younguns and..."

At the general store, the old men playing checkers went quiet as Grizzly and his bear entered. Grizzly greeted Charlie Boyer and got right to the point. "You got a letter here for me?"

Boyer knew that Grizzly was upset, but didn't figure there was any way to fib his way out of this. "Yup, got it right here. Was even thinkin' 'bout bringin' it to you myself and..."

Grizzly interrupted him. There was something about the man's tone that made him think that he was in for trouble. He quickly read the letter, then read it slowly a second time, trying to absorb the implications of what it meant to his life.

A nephew. Cody wasn't hardly in britches when I came West. Everyone in the family's dead except Cody and I. Last of the Adams', he thought, putting the letter down.

"Why you'd let Claw Wyler read this?" he asked.

"Didn't. He just grabbed it," Charlie said, shaking his head.

Grizzly knew that Claw would go after that wagon train, to get his nephew. Then he thought of the medicine on the train.

"What else did you tell Claw 'bout that wagon train?"

"Nothin'."

"Does he know anythin' 'bout any fever medicine comin' on those wagons?" Grizzly asked.

Charlie started to speak, but Claxton shouted out from the back. "He knows."

Grizzly turned. "You sure?"

"Sure as I'll never walk normal again," the crippled man said.

Longknife said good-bye to the children, then went to the hotel to find a room. Not seein' a clerk around, he banged on the bell. "Anybody home?" he called out.

A small Chinese man with thick glasses popped up from behind the counter. "Didn't hear you come," he said.

"And I didn't see where you come from either," Longknife said, looking over the counter. "Name's Longknife. You got a room for two?"

Longknife put down one of his last gold coins and took the key. "When my friend Adams gets here, he may have someone with him, but don't you mind, 'cause he'll just sleep on the floor," he said, thinking about Ben.

The desk clerk started to protest that he didn't run that kind of hotel, but he stopped when he saw the big knife on Longknife's leg. "Very good," he smiled.

"And we're gonna need us a couple of soaks so you see that hot tubs are brought to the room."

"All right," the man nodded.

Grizzly entered the hotel, still deep in thought about Cody Jackson Adams. The desk clerk had his glasses off so he didn't notice that Ben was a bear.

"Name's Adams. I'll be needin' a room for the night and I'll be eatin' upstairs."

The desk clerk bowed slightly. "Your room is already waiting, Mr. Adams, along with hot baths."

"You got a stable for my friend here to sleep in?"

Grizzly asked, looking down at Ben.

The desk clerk tried to focus but it still just looked like a squat, ugly man. "Your friend said bring your friend up to room."

"Is it okay?" Grizzly asked. Ben sat on his haunches and wrapped his paws around Grizzly.

"If it okay with you, it okay with me," the desk clerk sighed. As Grizzly and Ben walked towards the stairs, the desk clerk whispered to himself, "That ugliest, hairiest man I've ever seen. And the bearded one's been in mountains too long."

Grizzly found Longknife in the room and read him the letter.

All Longknife could do was shake his head and whistle. "Why didn't you tell me you had a nephew?"

"There are a lot of Adams in Massachusetts."

"But how many of 'em are you related to?" Longknife persisted. He saw the pained look in Grizzly's eyes and knew that he was bringing up a past best forgotten.

"I guess now just one."

"This boy comin' out?"

Grizzly nodded. "Cody Jackson Adams."

Then Longknife chuckled. "Guess you'll be needin' to add on to your cabin after all. You best be lookin' at that little honeybee princess back at the Diggers and..."

"Nothin' doin'. I don't need a wife."

"But you've got a boy to raise and..."

Grizzly slapped his hands together in anger. "I got a nephew comin' out here. And if I can keep Claw Wyler from gettin' him, then I'll figure out what to do with him next."

Longknife shrugged and put on his cap. "Suit your-self," he said, heading toward the door.

"Where you goin'?"

"Got me a little errand to do down at the store."

"Errand?"

"That's right. Got to find me some gifts for the Buffalo girls," Longknife chuckled as he left the room.

Grizzly went down to the kitchen and ordered dinner to be brought up to the room. He asked for a steak with potatoes for himself and five pounds of raw beef for Ben. The cook looked at him like he was a savage.

When the cook told the desk clerk about the order, the Chinese man wiped off his thick glasses and said, "Ugliest, hairiest man I'd ever seen. He was so ugly that he looked like a bear!"

Grizzly opened the door, looking for Ben, who peeked out from under the covers. "Get outta there," Grizzly said, shooing Ben out. The bear laid down behind the bed.

While waiting for dinner, Grizzly busied himself drawing a map, trying to figure which trail Claw would take to intercept the orphan train.

When dinner arrived, Grizzly tipped the cook, and called Ben. Ben gobbled down the five pounds of raw meat, then sat back and let out a long belch.

"I'd burp too if I'd just eaten five pounds of raw beef," Grizzly laughed. Ben crawled back behind the bed and went to sleep.

When the hot tubs were pulled into the room, Grizzly decided not to wait for Longknife and got into his tub.

Lathering up his hair, he slipped back down into the water, not noticing that Ben had snuck into Longknife's tub.

When he came through the door, Longknife was in a great mood. "Look what I bought you," he said, holding up a new pair of men's long underwear. Before Grizzly could answer, Longknife saw Ben in his tub.

"Get outta there!" he shouted, splashing water in the bear's face.

Grizzly chuckled. "Didn't know he'd gotten in."

Longknife was beside himself. "Lot of thanks I get payin' for the room and buyin' you some clean britches. You let that fleabag get in my soak tub."

"Just calm down and take a soak," Grizzly said, but Longknife was eyeing the water in the other tub very closely. "What's wrong?"

"Guess it's all right," he mumbled as he took his clothes off.

Longknife draped his buckskins over the chair, then got into the tub.

After they'd soaked awhile in silence, Longknife got serious. "Bad thing, Claw knowin' 'bout your nephew Cody comin' this way."

"God works in his own way. Guess he's testin' me," Grizzly said quietly.

Longknife looked at his friend. "Want me to Bone Up and see what's comin'?"

Grizzly shook his head. "Don't believe in fortune tellin'."

"This ain't fortune tellin'," Longknife said, "that's for Gypsies. Readin' the bones is African, didn't I tell you?"

"What's gonna be will be," Grizzly said.

"Then if you don't mind, I'm gonna read the bones later to see what's gonna be." Then Longknife turned and looked at his friend. "What you need is a woman."

"Don't need nothin' but myself," Grizzly said, closing his eyes.

Without thinking, he reached for the beaded choker that was always around his neck, then remembered it was on the dresser.

A breeze rustled the curtains, tinkling a wind chime somewhere in the night. Grizzly thought about Jessie Dillon, feeling something that he hadn't felt for a long time.

Doc called her Mrs. Dillon, so she's taken anyway, he frowned, upset with himself that he was thinking about a woman.

If I can save that nephew of mine and find him a good home, I'm gonna head off to a new place and make myself a home where no one will ever find me, he vowed.

CHAPTER TWENTY-ONE

Dead of Night

Across the valley, the big gray grizzly with the two missing toes watched quietly from the cover of the trees. It had been restless for hours, pawing the ground, pacing back and forth. But now Claw Wyler and his men were asleep and it was sure that the humans wouldn't be leaving until light.

Cody couldn't sleep. Sitting on the ridge looking down at the wagons, he wondered what Penny was dreaming about. *She's 'bout the prettiest girl in the world*, he thought, trying to figure out why his heart beat faster each time he thought of her.

He made sure that Runt was asleep then took off on a night stroll. *In the book Grizzly says that the woods come alive at night*, he thought, trying to test himself. He wondered if there were Indians in the woods, remembering the horror stories about Indian raids and scalping that the passing wagon trains shared with each other.

Can't let all that scare me, Cody gulped, taking a deep breath.

He heard wolves in the distance and almost bumped into an antelope and a deer drinking at a small creek. But the wolves howled again and the animals ran off into the darkness.

Cody knew that if he didn't come to grips with his fear, that he'd never live up to the standards he felt his uncle would set for him. And if he didn't get over his fear of the bogeyman, which he'd had since other kids picked on him at the orphanage, he'd never be a mountain man.

At the back of the knoll, Cody came to a swampy area. He listened to the frogs croaking in song, and tapped the water with his toe. The heavy, greenish scum that lay on the top broke into pieces in the moonlight.

"No such thing as the bogeyman," Cody whispered, trying to convince himself. An owl hooted from the trees, sending a shiver down his spine.

He found a path and walked along it, but soon lost his way. Cody spun around, trying to backtrack, but ran straight into a curling snake hanging from a branch. He panicked and ran, crashing through the undergrowth.

He started to yell for his ma then remembered that she was dead. "Oh God, get me outta here," he moaned, dodging the low-hanging branches and vines.

The light of the moon cast an eerie glow over the swamp. Running as fast as he could, swatting at bugs, Cody ran straight into an old man.

"Help!" Cody screamed, pushing Peepers away. He'd never seen a man with a hair and beard that long. He saw the man's tattooed chin and arms and figured he was the bogeyman.

"Hush," whispered Peepers, holding Cody at arm's length.

"Leave me alone," Cody exclaimed, struggling to get away. But the old man's grip was too strong.

"Who are you?" Cody whispered, knowing for sure that this strange old man had to be related to the bogeyman.

"Don't matter. Came to warn you that there are bad men nearby."

"Where?"

"Nearby," Peepers whispered. "But she's goin' to protect you."

"Who?" Cody asked, looking around. He followed the old man's pointed finger until he saw the bear.

"What is that?" he whispered, looking at the ghostly gray bear standing at the edge of the swamp. It seemed to be shimmering in the moonlight.

"It's a bear, a grizzly bear," Peepers said. "And she's been waitin' for you." He took Cody by the arm and pulled him forward.

Cody resisted, as if he was being pulled along in a bad dream. "Don't want to go," he moaned, but the old man was too strong.

"Here he is," Peepers said to the bear, letting go of Cody's arm.

The big bear with the two missing toes stepped forward, sniffing the air. Cody wanted to run, wanted to scream, but he was too scared to do anything but freeze in place.

"He ain't like them others," Peepers said to the bear. "He ain't like the bad ones up there."

Cody watched in frightened silence as the bear sniffed his legs, stomach and face. "She won't hurt you," the old man said, moving backward. "She's been watchin' over you, that's how I know."

Cody didn't notice that the old man had slipped away, disappearing into the bushes. The bear stared into Cody's eyes, as if it was reading something, then turned and walked back into the bushes.

Cody stood speechless, not knowing if he'd imagined what had happened in the dead of night. He finally found his way back to the sleeping Runt. For the rest of that night he dreamed of a big bear leading him on through the woods. He followed the bear in the eerie moonlight to the entrance of a cave.

CHAPTER TWENTY-TWO

On the Trail

Grizzly Adams was awake before dawn, dragging Longknife with him. He'd had trouble sleeping all night, having figured that the wagon train wasn't very far away.

"I'll be out front waitin'," he told the sleepy Longknife."

Longknife scratched his head. "This was the worst time I've ever had in a town. We didn't drink, gamble, or do nothin'."

"That's the way I like it," Grizzly said. "Ben, come," he commanded.

"Have them start some coffee," Longknife called out, "and not none of that acorn coffee neither."

Although he thought almost everyone would be asleep, the town was already alive with farmers bringing in goods. Doc Watters and Jessie Dillon were tending to the sick. When Grizzly saw Jessie, he turned away, hoping she couldn't read his thoughts. What little he remembered from his dreams had been about loving her.

Jessie went into Doc's office to get some bandages, which gave the two men a chance to talk. "What do you think of Jessie?"

Grizzly hesitated, knowing that some men would fight over talk about their wives. "She's a pretty woman. Lucky man who's married to her."

"Was lucky," Doc said, very matter-of-factly. "Buried him couple month's back, him and her son."

"She's a widow?" Grizzly asked.

"And I think she's takin' a shinin' to you," Doc said, "though what she sees in a man who lives with a bear is beyond me."

Longknife heard the last comment as he staggered out. "And it's beyond me too."

"You two goin' after that band of renegades by yourselves?" Doc asked.

Big Jake came up with carrying a rifle. "W...w...wait for me!" he said, trying to get on his coat.

"Almost forgot the troops," Longknife said.

"Who's he?" Grizzly asked.

"Name's Big Jake. Met him at the store last night. Said he wanted to come with us. Was the only one I ran into man enough to want to come along."

"Goin's gonna be rough," Grizzly said.

"He's got a reason to fight." Longknife took Grizzly aside. "Look, man lost his son to the Crows and he's worried sick. He wants to come do what he can. We're gonna need some help."

Grizzly hesitated and Longknife took that as acceptance. "You're comin', Big Jake."

"Think that'll be enough?" Doc asked.

"With Jake, that'll make five of us."

Grizzly looked around. "Five?"

Longknife grinned. "You, me, Ben, Jake, and..."

Grizzly Adams shook his head. "That's only four."

Longknife smiled, drawing his famous blade slowly out. "And this makes five," he said, holding it up. The light from the lantern on the hotel porch reflected off the blade.

Jessie came back over and Longknife caught the look

between she and Grizzly. "Are you leaving now?" she asked. Grizzly nodded. She handed them some fresh rolls she'd baked. "Eat these on the trail and come back safely."

Longknife put his hand on Grizzly's shoulder. "Grizzly Adams will be back. You can count on that, lady."

"Let's go," Grizzly said, embarrassed. Jake followed behind the two men and the bear. When they had gone a bloc, Grizzly scolded Longknife, "Why'd you tell her that?"

Longknife shrugged. "You got a nephew comin' out and I seen you makin' moon-eyes at that purty woman and..."

"I was not!"

"You were too," Longknife smiled. "'Besides, you're gonna need a wife if you're gonna raise a boy."

"I ain't raisin' no boy."

"That's not what the bones say," Longknife said, going nose to nose with his friend.

"How you know she's interested in marryin'?" Grizzly asked, disgusted that Longknife was meddling with his personal life again.

"I nosed 'round. She's a widow woman. She's as lonely as you are."

"I'm not lonely," Grizzly Adams huffed. "I've got Ben." The bear made a noise, pawing at Grizzly's leg. "We've been together a long time, haven't we, Ben?"

"That's what worries me," Longknife said, deadpan. As they headed east, Longknife joked, "And you best be changin' your name. Somethin' like Pappy Adams would be better, now that you'll be raisin' younguns 'stead of grizzly bears."

CHAPTER TWENTY-THREE

Attack

At the break of dawn, Thunder took the sacred ash from his medicine bag and uttered a prayer. Trapper watched, hoping that if anyone took a bullet, it would be Thunder.

"Ain't you finished yet?" he asked scornfully. Thunder ignored him, continuing with his prayer.

When he was finished, Thunder looked to Claw and nodded. "We're ready."

"It's 'bout time," Trapper said.

"Load up," Claw commanded. "Remember, no one hurt the children."

Trapper looked down at the wagons. "Figure you'll know what the fever medicine looks like?"

"I figure that those kids will tell me anythin' I want to know, includin' who's Grizzly's nephew."

"And what if they hold back on where the medicine is?"

Claw took out his knife. "I'll just have to cut one a bit until he talks. Believe me, those kids will talk."

They attacked at first light, hitting the lone driver who had risen to stoke a coffee fire. Thunder's arrow pinned him to the side of the wagon.

The other drivers were no match for the running Indians, who jumped into the wagons, stabbing and scalping the adults. The wagon master herded the children together in a desperate attempt to protect them, but he died in a flurry of shots.

The only adult to survive was Rev. Brice, who hid under the feed bags in the supply wagon. He wanted to help the screaming children, but he had heard so many Indian tales that he didn't have the courage to climb out.

Cody and Runt heard the commotion and crawled through the bushes to look. Below them, two of the wagons were burning and dead men lay where they'd fallen.

Even the two women who'd been along on the trip were dead, killed while protecting their wounded husbands. Only the orphans were alive.

"What are we gonna do?" Runt whispered.

Cody, who was still unclear about what had happened in the swamp, shook his head. "Just keep quiet," he said. The dream he'd had, of a bear leading him through the woods, kept coming back to him.

"Come on, Penny," he whispered, looking at the girl he liked. She saw where he was hiding and mouthed the word, *Run!*

But Cody shook his head and mouthed back, *Not without you.*

They watched as two white men came down from the woods to join the Indians below. Cody remembered what the old man had told him about bad men nearby and now knew what he had meant.

The boys were hidden under the bushes, laying on the cool earth. Runt felt something on his foot and turned around. What he saw made him feel faint. Standing behind them was the biggest bear he'd ever seen in his life.

He tapped Cody's arm, pointing behind. "What?" Cody asked. But all Runt could do was point.

Cody turned and saw the backside of the bear running through the trees. He blinked and the bear was gone. The only thing that remained was a strange looking bear print. Just like the dream he'd had.

Clay Wyler looked at the children. "Which one of you is Adams?" The two girls from Cody's wagon began crying. "Shut your mouth!" Claw said coldly, shaking one by the shoulders.

Claw walked slowly in front of them. The horrible scars on his face frightened the children into silence. "Which one of you is Grizzly Adams' kid?" he asked. Pete could hardly believe what he heard—it was confirmation of what Cody had been telling them since they left Boston.

From their hiding place, Runt and Cody kept quiet, watching. "Look at his face," Runt said. Claw Wyler was the scariest man he'd ever seen.

"Looks like a monster," Cody said.

"Think they're gonna scalp the kids?"

"Dunno," Cody shrugged, keeping his eyes on Penny.

Claw wanted to get it over with. "I'm talkin' 'bout Cody Jackson Adams. Which one of you is it?" he asked, but none of the children responded.

Runt looked at Cody. "They're lookin' for you. Is that your uncle?"

"No," Cody said, wanting to cuff his red-headed friend. "These men are bandits."

Trapper picked up one of the smaller children, a five-year-old boy, and drew his knife. "One of you better answer quick or I'll have to make this child 'bout a head shorter," he said, putting the knife to the child's neck. The boy began to cry.

Trapper pushed the knife against the boy's throat. "Someone better speak up quick 'fore I kill him."

Pete spoke up, holding his sore nose. "He ain't here."

"Where is he?" Claw asked, sticking his face up to Pete's.

Pete pointed up toward the stand of trees where the boys were sent. "Up there. He was sent to sleep up there."

Penny lifted her long dress and kicked Pete in the shins and Claw nodded. "That kick means fat boy here is telling the truth." He turned to Thunder and said, "Go get the boy."

Then he looked at Pete. "Where's the cholera medicine?"

Pete shook his head. "I don't know."

"Well one of you rats better know, 'cause the Crow Indians need it...like they need all you children." He walked between the kids, grinning. "Yes, sir, you children are going to make good Indian slaves."

Trapper walked up holding Rev. Brice by the scruff of his neck. "Look what I found hidin' like a scared rabbit. Bet he knows where the medicine is."

Thunder and one of the braves started up the hill just as the big bear came charging out from the woods. She caught the first Crow with a swipe of its talons, tearing at his buckskins and neck. The Indian dropped without a cry.

Thunder stood his ground, touching the medicine bag that hung from his waist, but the big bear passed by, going straight toward Claw.

"Watch out!" Trapper screamed, dropping his hold on the minister.

Claw got behind the children, using them as a shield, but the bear just circled around him. The children crawled under the wagon, trying to get out of the way.

Trapper aimed but the shot went wide, missing the bear, hitting the side of a wagon. Claw swung around, trying to find the bear, who came up under the wagon, turning it over as she reared.

"You want me?" Claw screamed, and the bear roared back, then turned and ran toward the woods.

"Stay here," Cody said to Runt. He got up and edged along the bushes. *That's the same bear. I didn't imagine things at the swamp.*

He kept an eye on Penny, who had managed to climb inside the supply wagon in the confusion. Cody made his way across the clearing, unaware that Thunder was moving swiftly behind him. "Watch it!" Runt screamed, running down to help his friend.

The bear turned and saw the Indian heading toward Cody and charged between them. Thunder backed off. Claw saw a resemblance between the boy and Grizzly Adams. "That's the kid!" he shouted. Trapper started after Cody.

Cody rolled beneath a wagon, trying to work his way over to Penny. "Gotcha," Claw said, coming up from behind him, but Runt climbed up on the wagon, picked up a shovel, and hit Claw on the head.

"Run," Penny shouted from her wagon. Trapper was coming right at the boys.

Cody and Runt rolled under the next wagon and beside Penny. "Come on," Cody said almost out of breath.

"Where?" she asked.

"To the woods," he said. "These men are gonna sell us all to the Indians."

Claw came up under the wagon and grabbed Cody's arm. "Not all, just them. You, I'm gonna kill along with that uncle of yours."

Trapper saw the returning bear first. He raised his gun and fired a shot, just grazing the big bear's head. Claw turned to look and Cody punched him in the stomach.

"Come on," Cody said, grabbing Penny's hand, pulling her along. The wind picked up the edge of her dress.

"Wait," she said, reaching back into the supply wagon. She brought out a leather satchel.

"What's that?" Cody asked.

"Medicine. It's for the doctor at the fort."

"She's got the medicine!" Rev. Brice shouted from beneath a wagon, worried about Claw's anger if the medicine was lost.

Claw raised his gun and fired, putting a hole in the wagon canvas between them. "Get 'em!" he screamed, but Trapper and Thunder were too busy trying to fight off the bear.

"Let's go," Cody said, taking her by the hand.

"What about me?" Runt shouted.

"Come on!" Penny screamed.

The bear covered the children's escape by knocking

down another Crow, crushing his windpipe.

"She's gonna kill 'em," Claw said, watching the bear chase after the three children.

"I don't think so," Thunder said, nodding as the bear raced past the children.

"Guess he's got a thing for bears," Trapper said, watching the bear turn and look back toward the three kids. "Just like his uncle."

"The bear could have killed you," Thunder said.

"I scared it off," Claw bragged falsely.

"Maybe your face did, but that grizzly left on its own accord," Trapper said. "And those kids got themselves a good headstart on us."

"We'll, find 'em," Claw said. "Loose those mules," he ordered Thunder, then turned to face the orphans.

"What you gonna do with them kids?" Trapper asked, nodding to the orphans. "Kill 'em or bring 'em along?" Claw looked at the orphans but didn't say anything. Trapper continued talking. "Mighty hard to track someone while draggin' along a pack of wet-noses."

Claw shouted to the Crows, "Loot the wagons for what they wanted, then burn them." He called Thunder. "Tell your brothers to take the orphans back to Bear Robe's camp. Tell them that we'll be bringin' Bear Robe some special fever medicine real soon," Claw said.

The wagons caught flame. The orphans huddled in a circle, convinced that the men were going to kill them.

"What about him?" Trapper said, looking at Rev. Brice.

Claw shrugged. "Just give him to Bear Robe as a slave."

"But the medicine," Rev. Brice said. "You must save the medicine."

"What for?" Trapper asked, wanting to smack the man across the face.

"Because...because the people of Fort Henderson need it."

Claw took the minister's arm and bent it backwards. "I don't give a damn about Fort Henderson. I care 'bout the Crows and killin' Grizzly Adams. You got that?"

Trapper cocked his head and turned in a slow circle. "You hear somethin'?" Claw asked, dropping the minister's arm and looking toward the woods.

But the only sound was the whimpering children and the wind that whipped down the hill. A fine film of snow fell softly around them.

"If we don't get those kids, the cold will," Thunder said.

"Gettin' them and keepin' them is two different things," Trapper said. Claw gave him a questioning look. "Between that big bear and Grizzly Adams, we got to get them fast."

"You think Adams is comin'?" Thunder asked.

"I *know* he's comin'," Trapper grunted. "He just seems to know things. Like the animals are tellin' him or somethin'."

Trapper frowned. "I just got a feelin' that we're bein' watched, that's all." An eagle circled overhead. "Like that thing there. I swear it's been followin' us since we burned down that settler's cabin."

Thunder watched the majestic eagle swoop behind the ridge, then back up. *He knows*, Thunder thought to himself. *The spirits are against us.*

Claw picked up his Sharps rifle and took aim, but as he fired the wind changed. The shot went wide and the eagle dove away out of sight.

Wolves howled in the distance and a cougar roared. Trapper's facial tic started jumping. "I tell you, there's animals everywhere, callin' out to Adams." He turned to Claw. "You saw the way he talked to the bear that ripped your face, didn't you?"

Claw slapped him. "You're losin' it."

Trapper licked at his lips where a trickle of blood had started. From up in the hills, the roar of the grizzly that had been following them echoed across the trail.

"She wants you," Trapper said. "She's been huntin' you, wantin' to kill you for shootin' off her toes. You know it's the same one, don't you?"

"Guess I just got to kill her too," Claw whispered, although he didn't sound sure of himself.

"You're going to get us all killed," Trapper hissed.

"Only the weak die, and I ain't weak," Claw replied.

Thunder fingered his medicine bag, praying to the spirits to protect him from the death he felt was in the air.

CHAPTER TWENTY-FOUR

Escape Through the Wilderness

Cody ran ahead, looking for the big bear, but it had vanished. *Saw my tracks and the bear's in the woods, in my dream*, Cody thought as he raced along. There was nothing in the dime novel about this so he was on his own.

"Keep an eye out for that bear," Runt said. "That thing could eat us all."

"She ain't gonna hurt us," Cody said.

"You sound pretty dang sure."

"Saw it in my dream," Cody said.

"Oh great," Runt moaned. "Now we're followin' a bad dream."

Penny saw the smoke of the burning wagons behind them and shivered. "They're gonna be followin' us, aren't they?" she said. Cody nodded.

"Where we goin'?" Runt asked, dodging a low-hanging branch.

"I'm followin' him," Penny said, holding onto the medicine satchel.

"Want me to carry that?" Cody asked.

"I'll manage," Penny said, lifting up her skirt to climb over a fallen tree. At the sight of her ankle, Cody turned away, blushing.

Cody led them through the woods, jumping over fallen trees, and scrambling over boulders. He remembered what the dime novel said about putting as much distance between you and your pursuers as fast as you could, and that was what he intended to do.

"They're gonna be hot on our tail," Cody said, when

they stopped at the edge of a small stream.

"We'll never outrun their horses," Runt said.

"Got no choice," Cody said. "Unless you want to be an Indian slave."

He stepped into the stream and ran up one side, climbed up the bank, shinned along a branch and dropped back down. Penny and Runt looked at him like he was crazy. "Now you two do somethin' like that on the rocks over there."

"Somethin' like what?" Penny asked, confused.

"Make double tracks. My Uncle Grizzly said that you always got to make double tracks to throw off Indians."

"Thought you'd never met him?" Penny said.

Runt moaned. "It's that dang book he's always readin'."

"You learned about that in a book?" Penny asked.

Cody held up the dime novel about his uncle. "Read it all in here."

"Guess I should learn to read," Runt mumbled, then he sneezed.

"Gettin' a cold?" Cody asked.

Run nodded. "Got it from sleepin' out last night without a blanket."

They ran along the ridges, keeping near the bushes, just as Cody figured his Uncle Grizzly would do. Cody knew from back East that the nip in the air meant a bad storm was coming. The snowflakes and flurries only confirmed his worst fears.

He also knew that if they didn't find shelter, the snow could kill them as easily as a bullet or an arrow. Using the sun as his guide, he calculated the direction that the wagons had been taking and the distance to Fort Henderson. He figured that if they could keep a quick pace, they could lose Claw and his men. But laying between them and the fort were miles of treacherous ridges, dangerous wolves, Bear Robe's camp, and the Crow hunting party. Getting safely through all of that would take a miracle.

Claw Wyler kicked the flanks of his horse. "Come on, keep goin'," he grumbled. The snow flurries were getting thicker now. Thunder dismounted and looked at the tracks. "They're running tired already."

"How can you tell?" Trapper asked, irritated by the Indian's tracking skill. The tic in his face was moving like it had a life of its own.

"Their steps are different. Some light, some heavy. Like they're running, not knowing where they're going."

When they got to the creek, it took Thunder twenty minutes to figure out what Cody had done. Trapper chuckled to himself, knowing that the game was changing. "Kid's layin' down fake tracks on us. I think we got ourselves a little badger."

"He has the blood of Grizzly Adams in him," Thunder said flatly, looking at the tracks with renewed respect.

"Just as long as that bear stays away," Claw said. His feelings toward the old bear had changed to fear. Claw was now convinced that the bear was like a bad hoodoo on him. A ghost bear that couldn't be killed, that had come to haunt him.

Grizzly and Longknife kept up a hard pace to make it to Squaw Pass. Big Jake did his best to keep up, but he wasn't used to the wilderness trails.

"S...s...sorry I'm h...h...holdin'" you up," Big Jake stuttered.

"Just do your best," Grizzly said, worried that the snow flurries would lead to a blinding snowstorm.

Freedom circled around twice, then flew off toward Squaw Pass. Grizzly saw the smoke from the burning wagons in the distance.

"Looks like we're too late," Longknife said.

"No time to waste," Grizzly said running ahead. He stopped short and held up his hand for silence. Longknife came up beside him. Grizzly nodded down to the ravine where the Crow Indians were herding a group of children and one adult.

Grizzly signaled for Longknife to go around and for Big Jake to stay put. Then he slipped quietly through the woods with Ben following.

Longknife waited for the command from Grizzly. As the Indians passed below them, Grizzly took one of the Indians down in a tumbling fall. Longknife cornered the other two, who came at him with their knives.

"Two 'gainst one ain't fair," Longknife said, drawing out his famous knife. "Now we're even."

While Grizzly fought with the other Indian, Longknife battled the two Crows. With his blade slashing like a reaper, Longknife cut the first Crow that charged. When both Indians jumped on him, they rolled down the embankment.

The children watched in horror. Rev. Brice wanted to run, but he stayed because the woods scared him. When an Indian tried to throw his knife at Grizzly, Ben rushed up and knocked him down. When he sat up, Grizzly held his Kentucky rifle against the Indian's neck.

"Finished?" he asked in the Crow's language, and the Crow grunted. Grizzly didn't want to kill him. He wanted to send Bear Robe a message.

He looked at the children and then at Rev. Brice. "Where's my friend?"

"Two Indians pulled him down the hill," Rev. Brice. "God rest his soul," he said, believing that Longknife was dead.

"Don't bury me so fast," Longknife said, coming up the hill, wiping his blade.

"Where are the Crows?" Grizzly asked.

"Let's just say they won't be causin' anyone no more trouble," Longknife said, putting his big knife back into its sheath.

Big Jake came running down the hill, thinking that his son might be among these children. "Sorry Jake," Longknife said, "these kids are from the orphan train."

After the frightened children calmed down, they told Grizzly about the attack on the wagons. Adams knew it was Claw's doing. He looked at the kids. He walked among them, eyeing their faces, then asked the minister. "Which one is Cody Jackson Adams?"

Pete spoke up. "He ain't here."

"Where is he?" Grizzly asked.

Ben sniffed at Rev. Brice and growled.

"He took the medicine and two other kids and ran for the woods," Pete said.

"Why didn't you all follow?" Longknife asked.

"'Cause Rev. Brice was punishin' them," a little girl said.

Grizzly looked at the minister. "Punishin' them for what?"

Rev. Brice cleared his throat. "Your, ah, nephew is a very headstrong boy."

"Just like his uncle," Longknife mumbled.

Rev. Brice continued. "He's always reading a picture book about you and..."

Longknife shook his head. "Seems everyone's read it but me."

"Enough," Grizzly said. "Did the man with the scarred face go after them?"

Pete spoke up. "Man with the ugliest face I ever seen and another white man, along with an Indian with scalps on his belt. They went after your...your nephew."

"Why you have trouble sayin' that?" Longknife asked.

Pete looked down, the scabs on his nose from the possum bite thick and prominent. "'Cause I didn't believe he was related to Grizzly Adams."

Longknife patted the boy on the back. "Some folks might say that's not such a blessin'." He looked at Pete's nose. "And you better be careful diggin' for gold 'cause you 'bout picked your nose clean off." Several of the children began to laugh.

A little girl looked at Ben, then tugged on Grizzly's buckskin pants. "Was the bear who saved us yours?"

"What bear?" Grizzly asked, startled

Rev. Brice looked at Ben then shook his head. "It was a different bear, bigger, gray color."

"Go on," Grizzly said.

"Strangest thing I ever saw. A wild bear charging in, fighting off them murderers like it was defending us."

Longknife looked at Grizzly and nodded. "Sounds like the ghost bear, Griz."

"I assure you that this bear was anything but a ghost," Rev. Brice said.

Longknife spat and reached into his carry-sack to tickle his ferrets. "Sounds like there's more than just three men followin' those kids."

Grizzly learned from the surviving Indian that they were followers of Bear Robe, the medicine man. The Indian said that Bear Robe needed the children to cure the white man's fever.

"Thought he was sellin' them to the Snake River Tribe," Longknife said. "That was the word 'round the rendezvous."

Grizzly translated and the Indian shook his head vigorously, telling Grizzly that Bear Robe had a new vision, with the white man's children being sacrificed to stop the disease the settlers had brought to the Crows.

"A...a...ask him if he knows where the stolen children are," Big Jake said.

Grizzly saw the pain in the man's eyes and asked the Crow. The answer was one of both hope and worry for

Jake. "The Crow said that Bear Robe has twelve white children back at his camp."

"Is my boy there?" Big Jake asked, holding up the picture of his son. The Indian looked, then shrugged.

"Let's go after my boy," Big Jake said.

"We'll go after 'em," Grizzly said. "But first we got a pack of kids here to take care of."

Grizzly sent the Indian back to Bear Robe with a message. "You tell your medicine man that I'll be comin' for the children." Grizzly could tell that the Indian wasn't impressed. "Tell him that I'll be bringing medicine to cure his people of the fever in exchange for the kids."

"But that medicine's for the Fort," Rev. Brice exclaimed, worried that his medicine-for-church deal would fall apart.

"There's 'nough to share," Grizzly said flatly, not wanting any discussion.

"That's if we get it before Claw Wyler does," Longknife said.

The Indian ran off yipping, his cries frightening some of the children who huddled around Big Jake. Grizzly looked at the man and said, "Jake, you and this minister here take the children back to Fort Henderson."

"Wh...wh...when are you goin' to get my boy?" Big Jake asked.

"If your boy's there, we'll get him back. But don't be gettin' your hopes up. There's a lot of other tribes been raidin' in these hills."

Big Jake handed Grizzly the picture of his son to

take with him. "In case you find any of those children a...a...alive."

After they'd sent the children on their way, Grizzly and Longknife headed over to the burning wagons. "Look at these bear tracks," Longknife said, pointing out the prints with missing toes.

"That bear must have been tryin' to get at Claw," Grizzly said, shaking his head. "But I never heard of a bear with a memory goin' after revenge like that."

"Maybe there's some things you don't know 'bout critters," Longknife said. "But it's strange that the bear didn't kill Claw. Ain't like he couldn't have done it from the way those kids were carryin' on."

They covered the dead bodies with rocks, then followed the tracks left by Claw and his men. The snow flurries were increasing and the temperature was dropping.

Claw led his horse down the narrow trail, trying to keep the tracks in sight. Trapper followed, unable to shake the feeling of impending doom. *Somethin' bad's gonna happen. I can feel it in my bones.*

Thunder brought up the rear, rubbing his medicine bag. *After we get the fever medicine, I will kill both these men and hang their scalps from my lodge pole. The tribe will sing of my coup for years.*

Up above, hiding against a rock ledge, the three children held their breath. Cody looked over and saw that Runt was going to sneeze. "Don't," he whispered frantically, but it was too late.

"What was that?" Claw shouted, looking around.

Trapper eyed the ledges above. "Sounds like one of them little varmints got hisself a cold."

"There," Thunder said, pointing. Penny's dress was flapping over the edge of the ledge.

Trapper fired off a warning shot that zinged between the rocks. "Stay right there or you're dead."

"This way!" Cody shouted, taking Penny's hand. They made their way up the face of the sheer cliff, not looking down. Trapper's rifle shots bounced around them, but they just kept going until they rolled over the top.

Exhausted, Runt snuck a peek at the men and a bullet just missed his head. "We gotta keep going," Penny said, holding the medicine satchel under her arm.

They ran along the cliff until they found a pass down through the rocks. Then they heard the wolves howling. Runt looked back in fright.

"Wolves!" he screamed.

"Faster," Penny said, but they couldn't outrun the hungry wolves.

Cody stopped at a bend in the trail. They'd come to a dead end. "You and Penny go ahead," he said. "Climb up those rocks at the end and get up to the ridge."

"What about you?" Penny asked.

"I'll be along," Cody said, "but I got to hold back the wolves."

Runt and Penny scrambled up the rocks just as the wolves rounded the bend. Cody picked up a branch and knocked the first wolf over the edge. Two more wolves lunged at him and it was all Cody could do to roll out of the way.

The two wolves came toward him from different directions, the way they would stalk a deer. Penny closed her eyes. "Please, God, help Cody."

Runt picked up a rock about half his weight. "Look out, Cody," he screamed and dropped the rock down at one of the wolves. The bouncing boulder made the wolf back off, giving Cody the chance to run to the cliff and start climbing.

Cody climbed as fast as he could, but his belt caught on a pine that stuck out from the rocks. "I'm stuck!" he shouted, kicking at the wolves leaping for his legs.

Runt tossed another rock but a half-dozen more wolves came running down the path. Penny handed Runt the medicine satchel, and began to climb back down.

"Where you goin'?" Runt shouted.

"To help him," she said, holding up her skirt to keep it from snagging.

"Go back," Cody screamed. He kicked at the wolf who was biting his shoe. "Don't hurt yourself, Penny."

"Can't let you just hang there and get eaten," she said. "Grab my hand," she directed, reaching out.

"Watch it!" Runt shouted. Another rock tumbled down the cliff, crashing into the wolf. Cody looked up and caught a fleeting glimpse of Peepers.

Cody took Penny's hand and pulled himself up so he could undo his belt. "Thanks," he whispered, their faces so close that he could smell her breath.

"Now we're almost even," she smiled, giving him a quick peck on the cheek.

Penny climbed ahead and Cody followed, digging his fingers into the cliff. "You made it," Runt said, hugging him as he reached the top.

"Barely," Cody said, trying to catch his breath.

"Who threw that last rock?" Runt asked.

"You wouldn't believe me if I told you," Cody said, looking around for the old man.

"It's gettin' cold," Runt shivered. He sneezed.

Cody looked around, trying to get his bearings. Runt sneezed again. *It is gettin' cold. The snow's pickin' up. If we don't make it to cover, we're gonna freeze out here*, Cody thought. He opened up the dime novel, but there wasn't anything in it about this situation.

"What's it say to do?" Runt asked.

"Looks like we're on our own," Cody said.

"Not quite," Penny said, pointing across the top of the cliff. The big gray bear was fifty yards away, moving in a slow circle.

"What's it doin'?" Runt asked.

Penny was perplexed. "It's dancin' in a circle, lookin' at you, Cody."

Cody watched, then said, "I think it wants us to follow it."

"Follow a bear?" Runt asked. "Don't even think your Uncle Grizzly would do that."

But Cody knew there was something between him and the bear, that the bear was trying to tell him something. "Come on," he said, taking Penny's hand. "I saw it in my dream."

About the time Big Jake led the children into Fort

Henderson, the Crow brought the message to Bear Robe, who was having another vision. He saw a boy and a bear walking toward a mysterious cave. Bear Robe looked at the frightened children, wondering if the medicine that Grizzly Adams spoke about was stronger than that which would come from sacrificing the children.

The one with the half-face is an evil man, Bear Robe nodded, knowing that Claw Wyler cared nothing for the Crow people. *He only wants to kill Grizzly Adams. He burns with evil. He burns with revenge that will only bring death to all who follow him.*

Grizzly Adams and Longknife followed the tracks of the hunters and the hunted, but the falling snow was quickly covering the trail. Ben sniffed along the trees, then stood and roared.

"Look here," Longknife said. It was a print with two missing toes. "Looks like that ghost bear of yours is followin' along also."

When they got to the creek where Cody had tried to trick Claw and his men, Longknife laughed. "This kid is layin' down double tracks." He looked at Grizzly. "Thought this was a city kid. Where'd he learn to do it?"

"Beats me," Grizzly shrugs.

"You Adams are all alike," Longknife mumbled.

A biting, chill wind whipped through the forest. "Come on," Grizzly said. "We got to get to 'em before Claw gets him."

"Or the snow does," Longknife said.

Grizzly gripped his rifle and looked at the mountains ahead. "We're 'bout to pass the point of no return. You can turn back if you want. You don't owe me," he said to Longknife.

Longknife nodded. "Ain't no future in the past," he said. "I'm coming with you."

CHAPTER TWENTY-FIVE

The Cave of the Ghost Bear

The big bear headed along the bottom of the ravine. The clouds hung darkly, threatening to unleash a blizzard.

The bear passed the white pines she used to keep the cubs out of harm's way when she foraged for food. The bear's territory embraced several square miles, which she defended against outsiders. And part of this hunting land was where Grizzly Adams had built his cabin.

The bear had lost her first cub when fighting the same men she had been following. But she sensed that the bearded man who took the male cub meant no harm, while never forgetting the smell of the man who had shot and wounded her.

There was something in this blond boy, something that recalled the bearded man. And that was why the bear led him along to her cave. Her last cub of the season was hurt and would die in the snows because it had been unable to forage for food.

The bear lumbered into the cave and padded softly across the bedding she had dragged inside to make a soft bed for the winter. Sitting in the center of the chewed-up branches and leaves was the cub with the broken leg. The gray bear nuzzled her cub, then went back outside to make sure that the children were still following.

Cody did his best to follow the bear's tracks, which led down the ravine and along a stream. He listened for the sounds of the woods, trying to identify the animals he'd read about.

At the edge of a small lake, he heard what sounded like a big animal in the bushes in front of them. "What's that?" Runt asked.

Cody turned. "It's the bear, come on," he said.

"No it's not," Penny whispered.

Cody turned. Staring him in the face was the first moose he'd ever seen. It was wading, belly deep, in the water, looking for plants on the bottom to eat.

"Should we run?" Runt whispered, but Cody shook his head. He knew that the moose could outrun and out swim them.

Then the moose started towards them. Penny and Runt lined up behind Cody. "You two move up the hill," Cody said.

"What are you gonna do?" Runt asked.

"I'm gonna stop this moose."

"With what?" Penny asked.

"With my brain," Cody said. "Now go on."

The moose dropped his ears back, flaring its nostrils. Cody stood motionless, trying to stare the moose down. The coarse hair on the back and neck of the moose stood on end, signaling an impending charge.

"Back, back," Cody whispered, but the moose kept coming, sticking its nostrils up against Cody's face. The moose had horrible breath but Cody didn't move.

"Leave," Cody commanded softly, and to his surprise, the moose backed away.

"Run, Cody," Runt shouted from the hill above, but Cody stood his ground. He stared down the moose, eye-to-eye for several minutes. Then he picked up a small branch and swished it at the moose, telling it to leave, but the moose didn't move.

The moose stomped twice, as if to charge, and Cody dropped to the ground.

"He's hurt!" Penny cried.

Runt shook his head. "I think he's got somethin' up his sleeve."

Cody lay still like he was dead, letting the big moose sniff all over him. Finally, thinking that Cody was dead, he went back into the water to forage for more bottom plants. Cody waited until the moose was behind the tall water plants, then he scampered up the hill.

"You're so brave," Penny said when he got to the top of the small hill.

"Just the way my Uncle Grizzly played possum in the book," he smiled.

They picked up the bear's tracks, trusting in Cody's dream, but as the winds picked up and the snow began falling thicker, Cody could feel the temperature dropping. Though he knew that the snow would cover their tracks, throwing off Claw and his men, it also meant that they needed to find cover for the night.

I hope my dream's not crazy, Cody sighed, brushing the snow from his hair.

"My pants are freezing," Runt complained. They'd gotten wet crossing a stream, but there was nothing Cody could do about it.

Penny walked along silently, carrying the medicine satchel, wondering if they would make it 'til morning.

They came to a cabin, which they quickly passed by on seeing the cholera warning sign.

The snow began falling harder. It was getting dark and Cody knew that he had to do something. *They're followin' me. I'm leadin' 'em. They're my responsibility*, he thought, looking at Runt and Penny. *We're gonna die unless we find shelter.*

Then he saw it. The old man was waving him on, pointing to the ground and then to a path leading up the cliff face. Cody blinked, brushing away the snow, and Peepers vanished.

"We'll take shelter there," he said, pointing at the cave.

"You want us to go in there?" Runt said.

"We need to get out of the cold," Cody said.

"But there's a bear in there," Penny whispered.

"Trust me on this one. I've got a feelin'," Cody said.

Runt shook his head. "I got a feelin' that we'd have been safer sleepin' in that cabin with the sickness."

"She's waitin' for us," Cody said.

"Who?" Penny asked.

"The momma bear. She's waitin' to eat us," Runt answered.

Penny looked at Cody. "Are you sure 'bout goin' in there?"

Cody nodded. "Sure as I can be."

"Then let's go," she said, "'cause it's too cold to be out here."

When they got to the cave, Runt didn't want to go inside. "I'll sleep out here," he said.

"You'll freeze," Cody said, doing his best to cover

over their tracks.

"Better to be a frozen kid than a bear's supper."

"Suit yourself," Cody said, running past the entrance to make it look like they'd climbed up the ridge. Then he stepped backwards in his own tracks and crawled into the cave. Penny followed behind and finally, as the wind began to howl, Runt relented and scurried on his hands and knees after them.

"Well I'll be," Cody whispered. There in the center of the cave was a middle-sized bear cub with a twisted leg.

"What's wrong with it?" Penny asked, watching as the cub painfully tried to move toward them.

"Looks like it's got a broken leg," Cody said.

"What are you gonna do?" she asked.

Cody picked up the cub. "Guess we'll take it with us in the mornin' and fix its leg."

Runt wasn't keen on the idea. He heard a noise behind them. His face paled at the sight of the gigantic mother bear, standing at the cave's entrance. The cub tried to run to its mother when Cody put it down, but it couldn't go far without crying.

Cody had read all about bears in the dime novel and knew how dangerous they were. He was suddenly face-to-face with one in real life, not in a dime novel story or a dream.

"Don't move," he whispered to Runt, who was too scared to answer. "It looks like the momma grizzly bear's come back."

"Hope your dream weren't no nightmare," Runt mumbled.

The mother bear came up and sniffed them all, but stared into Cody's face. Then she laid down to sleep right next to them with the cub curling up beside her.

"What should we do?" Penny asked.

Runt yawned. "I'm kinda tired."

"You two rest, I'll sit up and think of what we're gonna do in the mornin'." The warmth of the bear was like a big fur blanket and soon they were all asleep beside the bear. The children were so tired that they didn't notice when the bear got up and left the cave.

Claw and Trapper had followed the three children's tracks through the snow to the mouth of the cave. "They're in there," Trapper whispered.

Thunder sniffed the air. "Bear cave."

Trapper made a face. "You think those kids would be in a cave with a bear? They ain't in there."

Claw agreed. "Come on," he said, moving forward. They tied up the horses in a partially covered pine stand, then trudged up the rock path. Trapper went partway up the trail, finding a sheer drop-off at the end, and came back chuckling.

"Them kids are probably wedged in the rocks ahead, but they ain't goin' nowhere. Trail ends at a drop."

Claw entered quietly. "We need to make a fire," Claw said. "It's too damned dark to see anything."

Trapper shrugged. "If they're in here, they're back there somewhere. They ain't goin' far."

"They're not in here," Claw said, looking around the cave. "Their tracks went up the ridge."

"Why don't we keep after 'em?" Trapper asked.

"We'll make camp here," Claw said. "We'll probably find them frozen to death on the trail."

Thunder heard a sound and saw the mother grizzly standing at the cave's entrance. He fired a shot, but missed.

Trapper's gun misfired as the bear charged. Claw backed up, trying to aim, but the cave was almost pitch black. Then, without warning, the bear retreated and raced from the cave.

"Whooeee," Trapper exclaimed, knowing it had been a close call, "she's as big as a Kodiak!" he said, remembering the Kodiak bears he'd hunted in Canada.

"Make a fire," Claw ordered. Thunder gathered together brush and sticks and made a pile. Within a few minutes he had a nice fire going. The others took off their thick coats and joined him by the fire.

Deep inside the cave, Cody awoke to the sound of the men's voices. He woke Penny and Runt, signaling them to be quiet. Runt started to sneeze, but Penny held his nose. "Thanks," he whispered, then gasped again. But just as he sneezed, the men laughed. They hadn't heard the sneeze.

The warmth of the fire put the men to sleep. Cody waited until he was sure they were snoring, then crawled forward and stole one of their big buffalo coats. He pulled it back and put it over the three of them and the cub.

"You want us to go to sleep?" Runt asked.

"No, we're gettin' outta here," Cody said. "Bring the medicine, Penny."

They crawled slowly along the side of the cave, trying not to wake the men. Cody saw the pistol sticking out of Trapper's pack and stuck it under his belt.

Runt's foot slipped out from under the coat as they crawled along and knocked the strap of Trapper's powder flask. Cody saw the smoldering strap and the flames moving towards the powder.

"Move fast!" he said, picking up the bear cub and running toward the entrance to the cave.

"What the hell?" Trapper said, sitting up with his rifle ready. He saw the powder flask near the fire and rolled out of the way. The flask exploded with a deafening roar.

Penny and Runt were knocked down by the blast, but Cody pulled them up. "We got to run 'fore they catch us," he said, pushing them forward. The bear cub was heavy but Cody wasn't going to leave it for the men to kill.

Claw came running out, his hair still smoldering. He raised his gun and fired at the children, but missed. Thunder emerged, his long hair nearly burned off, grimacing at the pain from the burns on his neck.

Trapper staggered out, his hearing nearly gone, but quickly got his bearings. He saw that the kids were running up the trail to where the drop-off was.

"We got 'em now," he said, taking out his knife.

On the other side of the ravine, Grizzly Adams heard the explosion and the gunshot. "They're right up there," he said, pointing toward the hill.

Ben roared and was answered by another bear. "Sounds like a lot of things are up there," Longknife said.

"Hurry up," Grizzly said, racing ahead of Longknife and Ben. They found the horses in the pine stand under the cliff and then came to the cave. Ben stayed behind to sniff at the familiar bear smell.

Trapper stepped on their tracks, grimacing at the pain from his burns. "I want to kill them," he mumbled to Claw. His tic was twitching uncontrollably.

"You kill the girl; I want Grizzly's nephew," Claw said.

Thunder followed behind. He'd heard the bear roar across the ravine and the other bear that answered. The Crow Indian knew that their fate had been sealed, and made the decision to kill Trapper when the opportunity arose.

Trapper pushed ahead through the night snow, wanting to be the first to take blood.

Cody looked down over the ledge. "We're trapped," he whispered.

"What should we do?" Penny asked, hearing the men approach. She clutched the medicine satchel like it was a life raft.

"Just get ready to die," Trapper growled, stepping up to them.

Cody moved protectively in front of Penny and Runt. "Leave them alone. They done you no harm."

"Don't matter to me what I kill them for. I'm just tired of tracking you," Trapper said, swinging his knife from side to side.

Claw came up and looked at Cody. "You must be

Adams' nephew, ain't you?"

"So what if I am?"

"Just wanted to make sure I was killin' the right one," Claw said. He turned to Thunder and said, "The girl's yours. Just make sure you don't hurt the medicine none."

Cody put the cub down and drew the pistol. "Leave us alone."

Trapper laughed. "Little thief stole my pistol," he said, moving forward. "Gonna cut you bad for doin' that. Then I'm gonna skin that cub."

Cody had never shot a gun before, but he drew back the hammer like it said in the dime novel and aimed. "Don't make me do this," he said, looking Trapper in the eye.

"I ain't makin' you do nothin', boy, except gonna make you die."

Cody pulled the trigger and shot Trapper in the gut. The blast sent Cody backwards, knocking down Runt and Penny and saving their lives, because Claw's shot passed right over them.

Trapper held his bleeding gut and staggered forward. "Gonna make you pay, boy."

Grizzly Adams came up from behind them, pointing his Kentucky rifle. "It's over."

Claw turned. "So we meet again, Adams," he said, pointing his Sharps rifle at Adams.

Longknife came up with his rifle cocked. He looked at Thunder. "Evenin', chief, any chance you wanna do some ferret leggin'?" he mocked. "Or maybe have me Bone Up and see what the future holds for you?"

"Is that Grizzly Adams?" Runt whispered to Cody.

"It's my uncle," Cody said, hardly believing his eyes.

Trapper made a quick move and grabbed Penny by the skirt. "I'll kill her," he threatened, putting his knife to her neck.

"Watch the ledge," Claw said, seeing that Trapper was getting close to the edge. Trapper turned to look.

In one fluid movement, Longknife dropped his rifle, drew his blade and threw it into Trapper's back. Cody grabbed Penny from Trapper's grasp as the man staggered backward, trying to pull the knife from his back.

Thunder took his medicine bag, squeezed it, and threw his knife at Longknife, hitting his bone bag. Longknife felt the thud of the knife.

He looked down. "Them are my bones," he said. Thunder watched in fear as Longknife's fortune telling bones poured out.

"You're a witch," Thunder whispered.

"And you're a bad thrower," Longknife said, taking out a broken rib bone from the bag and holding it up.

Terrified by Longknife's apparent spiritual powers, Thunder ran toward Trapper, pushing him over the cliff. Cody watched them drop into the darkness. Longknife shrugged, scooping up the bones. "Guess he didn't want his future told."

Claw charged toward Grizzly, knocking him to the ground. They rolled between the rocks, knives out, but neither could cut the other. Claw kneed Grizzly in the gut and staggered off down the trail.

"Let's go after him," Longknife said, cleaning off his blade.

"Ben's down there," Grizzly said.

Claw raced down the trail, figuring he'd find another rifle in the cave and then escape on his horse. The explosion had scattered the fire all over the cave.

"Got to be a rifle in here somewhere," he said frantically, searching through the cave.

Then he stopped. He could hear the labored breathing of a big animal. He sniffed the bear's presence.

Claw spun around and saw Ben Franklin in the entrance. "Adams, get your bear away from me!" he shouted, preferring to face Grizzly's gun rather than be eaten by the bear.

"Ben, come," Adams shouted, and the bear pulled back.

"I'm comin' out," Claw shouted. "I'm gonna get on my horse and ride outta here. You got the kids and the medicine, that's what you come for." Then he heard the breathing again. There was something else in the cave.

Ben danced in a half-circle, trying to tell Grizzly something. "What's in that cave, Ben?" Grizzly asked.

Claw moved toward the cave's entrance, feeling his way in the dark, and ran right into the arms of the grizzly bear. She picked him up in her paws, mauling at his face. Grizzly heard Claw's screams and took a step forward, but Longknife held his arm.

"Let things be as they be," he said. "That's what the bones said," he grinned.

Grizzly turned and looked at his nephew. "So you're Cody Jackson Adams," he said admiringly.

Cody tried to stick out his hand, but the cub was

struggling too much. "Pleased to meet you, Mr. Adams."

"And who are these two?" Longknife asked.

Cody introduced his friends. "This here's Runt and this lady's name is Penny."

Grizzly caught the look that passed between them. "Pretty girl you are, Penny," he said, taking the medicine bag from her. "This is going to save a lot of lives." She blushed, not accustomed to compliments.

Ben came up and sniffed at the cub. "Guess he likes the cub," Grizzly smiled.

Cody looked between the bears. "Didn't know that kodiaks and grizzlies got along."

"Kodiak?" Grizzly laughed.

"That's right. I know what I'm talkin' about," Cody said defensively.

Grizzly sighed. "I'm not young enough to know it all like you, son. That's a grizzly cub."

"It is?" Cody exclaimed. "Why, I heard that man who..." he paused, looking back to where Trapper had gone over the cliff.

"Who, what?" Grizzly asked.

Cody cleared his throat. "Why, I heard that man say that the momma bear was as big as a Kodiak."

Grizzly laughed. "Cody, that's just an expression that a lot of the mountain men use."

Longknife nodded. "That there's a grizzly cub with a hurt leg in your arms." Grizzly took the cub from Cody's hands and examined it.

Cody opened up the dime novel and shook his head. "You're right. It's a grizzly cub," he said proudly, pointing to the picture.

Longknife grabbed the dime novel. "Where you see that?"

Grizzly took it from him, handing it back to Cody. "Longknife can't read."

"Neither can Runt," Cody said, nodding toward his red-headed friend.

"They both need schoolin'," Grizzly Adams laughed, thinking about Jessie Dillon.

"We better head back toward Fort Henderson," Longknife said. "We'll put these kids on the horses and we'll make good time."

Grizzly and Ben started down the ridge. Longknife looked at Cody. "Your name is Cody Jackson Adams, right?" Cody nodded. "Well, from now, on I'm gonna call you Kodiak Jack," he smiled, "'cause of that Kodiak bear cub you got."

"Is that how Grizzly Adams got his name?" Cody asked.

"Don't it tell you all that in that book?" Longknife asked, winking at Grizzly Adams, who'd stopped to listen. Cody shook his head. "Well," Longknife smiled smugly, "some things you learn by readin' and some by listenin' and doin'."

Penny came and stood by Cody. Longknife put his arm on Runt's shoulders. "Come on...Runt," he said. "Guess you're walkin' with me."

As they walked off, Longknife said, "Runt, you're gonna have to tell me what that book says 'bout Grizzly Adams."

Runt shrugged. "Don't know how to read."

"Oh that's right. Well, you just got to tell me every-thin' you know 'bout these Adams from Mass-ass-chu-setts. By the way, are you a shoemaker too?"

Penny pulled Cody back behind a rock ledge and kissed his lips. "I hope that's your first kiss, Kodiak Jack."

"It...it is," he said, caught off guard.

"And I don't want no other girl ever kissin' you," she said, walking quickly to catch up with the others.

"Come on, Kodiak Jack," Longknife called out. He'd seen the smooch and grinned. "Or should I call you Romeo?"

"What are you talkin' 'bout now?" Grizzly asked him.

Longknife shrugged. "You just be thinkin' 'bout those Buffalo Girls and how warm they'd be on a cold night like this."

"Don't you ever get tired of talkin'?" Grizzly asked.

Longknife shook his head. "Just can't wait to see you raisin' Cody from an acorn to a real nut like you," he laughed, and began singing "Yankee Doodle."

"I ain't raisin' nobody, Grizzly thought, wondering what he was going to do with Cody.

As they made their way along the trail, Cody thought he caught a glimpse of an old man standing on the ridge in the moonlight. *Thanks for saving our lives,* Cody whispered, waving good-bye.

CHAPTER TWENTY-SIX

Grizzly Adams and Kodiak Jack

The town welcomed Grizzly Adams and his band like heroes, with a Thanksgiving feast that no one would forget. The orphans had been saved and the cholera medicine would protect the town.

During dinner, Grizzly knew that everyone was wondering if he was going to take Cody Jackson Adams back to his cabin and raise him. He didn't like being put on the spot.

I don't want the responsibility, he grumbled to himself. *I left civilization behind. Bad enough Longknife hangin' 'round, talkin' all the time. Now bring this boy with me? Who am I to raise a youngun?*

Longknife leaned over. "You gonna take the boy or what?"

"Don't know," Grizzly said.

Longknife felt in his bone bag, took out a handful of bones and looked at them. Then he glanced at Grizzly and Cody and put the bones back.

"Freedom, freedom, freedom," Longknife said. "That's all you ever think about."

"I just want my liberty," Grizzly said, "to be left alone like I leave others alone. To live my life like I want to."

Longknife shook his head. "You just want freedom from responsibility," he said, walking away.

After the Thanksgiving feast, Jessie Dillon asked the families of the town who had asked for orphan children to meet at the church. Doc Watters and Rev. Brice helped decide who the lucky new parents would be.

Longknife stood holding one of the three children that he and Grizzly had brought to the stable owners to raise. Big Jake and his wife stood in the back of the room, watching, wishing they had their boy back.

The new parents stood behind the child selected for them as the Rev. Brice went down the line of orphans. They all found waiting homes, even Pete, who was taken in by Charlie Boyer, who needed a hand at the general store.

Rev. Brice saved Penny, Runt and Cody for last, trying to get back at them by making them sweat. Jessie looked at Penny, wishing she was hers.

Doc Watters knew that Jessie wanted a child and had spent several hours convincing Rev. Brice that he should go along with it.

"And Penny," Rev. Brice began, "you are going to live with..." He paused, then turned. "With Miss Jessie Dillon."

Jessie was overjoyed and took Penny into her arms. Rev. Brice turned to Runt. "And Runt..."

"That's not my name," whispered the small, red-headed boy. "It's Edwin."

"All right...Edwin..." Rev. Brice said, drawing out the agony.

Runt had worried all night. Cody had his uncle and now Penny had a mother. All the families that had asked for children had gotten an orphan. Runt was the last one left. *No one wants me*, he thought, his lip beginning to quiver.

Doc Watters looked over at Big Jake and nodded. "Come get your new son," he grinned.

Big Jake rushed up and picked up the boy, who was dwarfed in his arms. "Hello, Edwin Runt," he said without stuttering.

"I ain't never had a daddy 'fore," Runt said, bursting into tears.

"I'm...I'm...I'm your daddy forever now," Big Jake beamed.

Then Rev. Brice turned to Cody. He looked the boy over, not wanting to acknowledge what a hero he was, then looked toward Grizzly Adams.

"You gonna take Cody Jackson Adams back to your cabin?"

"I live by myself," Grizzly said.

"Not anymore!" Longknife shouted. He handed the child to the stable owner and stormed forward.

"You're takin' him!"

"It's my decision," Grizzly said flatly.

"Then make the right one," Longknife said flatly. "I've seen what the bones say."

"I don't care 'bout your bones," Grizzly said, frowning.

Grizzly looked at Cody, then out the window. *I'm a loner. I live by myself. I can't be raisin' no boy. What do I have to teach him?* There was a long pause as everyone in the room held their breath. Cody closed his eyes and crossed his fingers, watching his uncle concentrate.

"Oh go on, Griz," Longknife said. "You can't stay an ol' sourpuss all your life."

Cody cleared his throat. "You do what you want to do, Uncle Grizzly," Cody said, "I'll be all right."

"Don't be sayin' that," Longknife warned, "or he's likely to sneak off without us."

Grizzly looked at the boy and knew what he had to do. "Cody Jackson Adams is comin' with me," he said.

"I am?" Cody stammered. Grizzly nodded. "I am!" Cody shouted, jumping up and down, whooping with joy.

Jessie grinned and took Grizzly's hand. "You made the right decision."

"I hope so," Grizzly sighed, knowing that his life was changing forever.

Runt looked at Cody and said, "I'll miss you."

Cody leaned over and said, "No matter what, we'll always be wilderness brothers forever."

"Forever," Runt grinned, grabbing Cody's hand the way they'd done in the woods.

"Come on, Edwin," Big Jake called out.

"Gotta go," Runt said. "My Pa's callin' me."

Penny walked over and held Cody's hand. "When will I see you again?"

Cody shrugged. "That's up to my uncle."

Big Jake came up and looked into Grizzly Adams' face. "Are you gonna get my boy back?" he asked.

"I'm gonna try, Big Jake, but I can't promise nothin'," Grizzly said.

"Do your best," Big Jake said.

Grizzly looked him in the eye. "I give you my word on that," Grizzly said and Big Jake walked off, satisfied.

Grizzly waved Kodiak over to him and said, "I didn't ask for this responsibility, so if you're gonna come along, you got to carry your own weight."

"I will, Uncle Grizzly," Cody beamed.

"And don't call me Uncle Grizzly. Sounds like a carnival man or somethin'."

"Uncle James?" Cody said, hesitantly.

"No, not Uncle James, neither. Left that name a long time ago." He thought for a moment, then walked off. "Just call me Griz or Grizzly. That'll do."

"Okay....Uncle...Griz."

Outside, Grizzly walked over to the side of the building. "Ben, come," he said, and Ben Franklin came out carrying the smaller bear by the nape of its neck.

"What are you gonna call your bear?" Grizzly asked Cody.

"I kinda like my own name but I kinda like the name Kodiak Jack. So I was thinkin' 'bout callin' the bear Cody and me Kodiak Jack."

"You think you're a mountain man or somethin', Mr. Kodiak Jack?" Grizzly laughed.

"I'm gonna be," Cody said, standing his ground.

"You got a lot to learn, tenderfoot," Grizzly said, pulling at Cody's store-bought shirt.

"I'll learn anythin' you wanna teach me 'cause I wanna make you proud." Ben came up and nuzzled against Cody and the boy hugged his neck like he was squeezing a lap dog. The cub whined for some of Cody's attention.

Grizzly watched and felt something. Though he wasn't sure yet what he was going to do with the boy, he knew that Cody Jackson Adams had the power over animals too. He'd seen it in the way he handled Ben and the bear cub and from the stories that Runt and Penny had told him about the way he'd stared down the big bear.

That afternoon, Grizzly, Longknife, and Cody brought the cholera medicine to the Crow's camp. There was enough for both the town and the Indian tribe, and Grizzly Adams had given Big Jake his word that he'd find his boy if he was still alive.

After Bear Robe had heard about the death of Claw, he knew that the vision was right. He looked at the boy standing next to Grizzly, the one with blond hair, and knew it was the same boy from his dream.

"He has the way with animals, like you do," Bear Robe said.

Grizzly nodded. "But he has to learn how to use it," Grizzly said.

Bear Robe accepted the exchange and opened the pen for Grizzly to enter. A dozen dirty, cowering children stared up at him. Grizzly looked at the picture that Big Jake had given him and picked up the small boy that he knew was Jake's son.

"Come on, kids," he said to the stolen children. "It's time to go home." Grizzly Adams had kept his word to everyone.

Big Jake waited at the edge of town and ran forward as Grizzly brought back the children. Runt watched as his new father hugged his blood son, feeling hurt and left out.

Big Jake walked back and leaned down to pick up Runt. "Meet your brother," he said. Runt felt like his heart would explode with happiness.

Jessie saw that Grizzly wanted to leave and walked over to him. "When will you be coming back?" she asked.

Grizzly started to say next year, but by the tone of her voice, he knew there was something there. "I'll be back soon, Jessie," he said, looking into her eyes.

"I'll be waiting," she whispered, kissing him on the cheek. Then she turned and walked away.

Penny made sure no one was looking and kissed Cody on the cheek. "And so will I," she whispered, squeezing his hand before she ran off to join her new mother.

Longknife pulled Grizzly's arm. "What am I gonna tell your little princess honeybee? You know how jealous she's gonna be?"

"Who?" Grizzly asked, absentmindedly, watching Jessie walk away.

"The Buffalo Girls. Why, we were gonna have a double wedding and..."

"Don't you ever stop talkin'?" Grizzly said. "Ben, move," he directed and walked away. Cody raced to catch up, carrying the cub under his arm.

Longknife double-stepped after them. "Guess I better get to readin' the bones, to see what the future holds," he said. He reached into his bone bag and took out a handful.

"What do they say?" Cody laughed, watching Longknife concentrate on the bones.

"They say that your uncle's always gonna be a stubborn cuss and that you're gonna be a mountain man."

"I'm gonna try," Cody said, "but I ain't never seen a

mountain man in city clothes." He looked at the tattered buckskins Longknife was wearing. "That's what I need, some buckskins," he sighed. The bear licked his ear.

"Maybe the bones got somethin' to say 'bout that," Longknife grinned. *And maybe I'll see if the Buffalo Girls can give the bones a little help.*

"Is that your eagle?" Cody asked Grizzly, pointing to the sky.

Riding the wind like a free spirit without boundaries, Freedom swooped down then flew away. "He comes 'round but no one owns Freedom," Grizzly replied.

Then Grizzly spotted a familiar gray shape. On the ridge above them, the big gray bear watched her two cubs. One was full-grown and one was just a baby. But they were both with the humans who had the look in their eyes. They both were humans who could live with bears.

Grizzly bowed slightly to the bear, who raised up and roared across the valley. "That's the bear I was tellin' you 'bout," Cody said.

"She was watchin' out for you," Grizzly stated.

He watched the bear walk back into the woods and thought again of his wilderness prayer. *That's God's path in the pathless forest. There is no loneliness in the lonely woods.*

Grizzly Adams and Kodiak Jack were heading for the edge of civilization. Two people, one a man who'd seen it all and one an orphan boy who wanted to learn the ways of the woods, were going off to live in the wilderness and become legends across America.

"I'm gonna do my best," Cody whispered to Longknife, "to learn from my uncle and make him proud."

"You'll do all right," Longknife said, tousling his hair.

"Hope the bones get me some 'skins," Cody said, looking down at his store-bought pants.

Longknife took a breath and began. "You ever heard of a crocollo?" Cody shook his head. "The meanest, the most dangerous creature in the world and it lives in Africa."

For the next hour, Longknife told whoppers to Cody as they walked along and Grizzly Adams was happy that Longknife had found someone else to talk to. When they got to the Digger Indian village, Longknife said good-bye and went to visit his Buffalo Girls.

The next morning, when Cody woke up in Grizzly's cabin, he found a pair of buckskins that were his size sitting on the front rock. On top of them was a bone handled knife which was inscribed, *Kodiak Jack*.

Thomas L. Tedrow

Thomas L. Tedrow is a best-selling author, screen-writer, and film producer. He prides himself on writing stories that families can read together and pass on to friends.

Promoting the concept that good books drive television and films, Tedrow's eight-book series, *The Days of Laura Ingalls Wilder*, is the basis for a television series. *Grizzly Adams and Kodiak Jack* is part of a series of Tedrow books and concepts designed to promote family reading and film entertainment.

Tedrow has a degree in Journalism/Public Relations from the University of Florida. He lives with his wife, Carla, and their children in Winter Park, Florida. He occasionally can be found in the wilderness...if you know where to look.

j   Tedrow, Thomas L.
TED

The legend of Grizzly
Adams and Kodiak Jack

63.409

2/13 1/14